Émile Zola, Alexander Teixeira de Mattos

The Heirs of Rabourdin

A Comedy in Three Acts

Émile Zola, Alexander Teixeira de Mattos

The Heirs of Rabourdin
A Comedy in Three Acts

ISBN/EAN: 9783337127664

Printed in Europe, USA, Canada, Australia, Japan

Cover: Foto ©Andreas Hilbeck / pixelio.de

More available books at **www.hansebooks.com**

THE HEIRS OF RABOURDIN. A COMEDY IN THREE ACTS BY EMILE ZOLA. TRANSLATED FROM THE FRENCH BY A. TEIXEIRA DE MATTOS.

LONDON: HENRY AND CO. BOUVERIE STREET, E.C. 1894

The Editor's Preface.

THE production of *The Heirs of Rabourdin* was a mistake. I own it frankly, adding that I alone am the culprit.

But the selection of this play was not a vulgar error of judgment, nor was it the result of thoughtless impulse.

I had good and sound reasons for resuscitating this farce, which (in so far as English people knew) had been slumbering for twenty years in well-deserved oblivion.

In the first place I like the play; I think it clever, simple, direct, humorous, though much spun out and harping on one string.

That is simply a matter of opinion.

Secondly: the play was not tried under favourable circumstances in France; it was produced at the Théâtre Beaumarchais—a, what we would call, transpontine theatre.

Thirdly: the very fact that the play was demolished with fury in Paris clearly proves that partiality had its hand in the game. Zola had not for nothing written feuilleton after feuilleton of mordant theatrical criticism. They were waiting for him, and when, the bold man that he is, he came forward with this farce, they turned their pens into clubs and struck at him.

Fourthly: twenty years later, the public of two great cities of Germany and Holland, the inhabitants of which are known to be as discriminating as they are severe, had greeted the revival of the play with genuine and ringing applause; while critics of established competence and fairness had reversed the judgment of their Parisian colleagues.

Fifthly and lastly: I was curious to know whether Molière's style of playwriting would meet with favour here, since the very lukewarm reception extended in London to his most popular play, *Le Malade Imaginaire*, had created some·doubt in my mind.

The Heirs of Rabourdin is avowedly a play *à la* Molière clothed in modern garb. If it had succeeded, I should have included *Les Précieuses Ridicules* in my next year's programme.

But the play has foundered, and I am almost convinced that even the very best of acting would fail to obtain for Molière's style a decree of naturalisation in England.

This is my case.

As regards the judgment passed by some of our critics on the selection of the play and the performance, I cannot help saying that it was unnecessarily harsh and vindictive.

Personally I do not mind : ever since I started the Independent Theatre I have encountered such cruel injustice in certain quarters that the evident *parti-pris* rather amuses than hurts me.

But I regret that actors who have done their best should have been made, in a certain sense, to serve as scapegoats for my mistake.

And, after all, was there really any need for such

torrents of abuse and for such rejoicings over a fiasco?

Theatrical management, pre-eminently dependent upon the mood of the multitude, has never been conducted without the commission of an error now and again. The elements of success on the stage are of so strangely composite a character that it is beyond human wit to blend them harmoniously at each and every attempt.

At any rate, there is this great difference between my mistakes and those of the ordinary manager :

My mistakes damage me alone ; his cost many people their employment.

And thus, with no pangs of conscience to torment me, a failure spurs me on " Excelsior."

J. T. GREIN.

LONDON, *March 5th,* 1894.

The
Author's Preface.

❧

I HAVE read carefully all that the critics have
written on *The Heirs of Rabourdin*. I was
anxious for instruction. I was prepared to
correct myself of the faults which should be
pointed out to me. I hoped to receive a profitable
lesson, advice prompted by experience, a complete,
well-reasoned, and judicial analysis of my dramatic
case. And see, I have received the most abominable
drubbing imaginable. Bludgeon blows did duty for
arguments. One bit at me, another threw his pen
between my legs to bring me down, while a third
split open my skull with blows of his fist from behind.
The common-sense critics cried : "Kill him !" and
the romanticist critics replied : "Knock him on the
head !" Ah ! you want to know what we think
of you, you wish us to pronounce judgment on your
work, you ask us for a well-grounded opinion ! Well,
then ! here is a trip of the heels for you, and here is
a storm of thumps on the head, and here a few
kicks in the ribs. That is complete : I am now
sufficiently enlightened.

I confess that, at first, this reception dumfoundered
me. It was not a discussion, it was a massacre.

Assuredly a novice, fresh from his village, landed at the theatre with some dramatic prodigy, would not be received with such hootings. He would be allowed, at least, some small particle of talent, he would be left some hope. As for me, I was seized, sentenced, and executed ; nothing remained for me but to lie prone upon the fragments of my play and to sham death. Our great dramatic criticism, which, as everybody knows, is the envy of the outside world ; this school which maintains public taste at so high a level, and, fulfilling its part of the good counsellor, has already endowed France with many a playwright of genius ; this literary institution, in short, drove me from the stage with one blow from its impeccable ferule. For twenty-four hours I remained bruised from my beating, hanging my head, very shamefaced, asking myself whether I would ever dare to reappear in public.

And yet, in spite of my religious respect for the critics, there commenced to awaken within me a desire to understand. I was smashed, pulverised, done for, destroyed : that was certain ; I had neither style, nor ideas, nor talent of any description : I was the first to grasp that ; but, after all, I should have wished for something less summary, for a word of explanation, a word for future guidance. Did the critics expect to close the theatre to me for ever ? I fear so. I re-read the articles, I thought them over, and I confess that I should be giving evidence of deplorable obstinacy were I to try anew my fortune on the boards. Not one extenuating circumstance was put forward. I was deprived of the consolations granted to the lowest of unsuccessful mimographers.

A hustling—nothing better. You are in the way ; get out of that. And, above all, don't come back. There are Pan-pipe poets, manufacturers of plays at so much per act, shady authors, who are born, it would seem, to write for the stage. I, no. When I make an attempt, I commit so monstrous a misdeed that they speak of leading me to the nearest police-station. If all that has been written on *The Heirs of Rabourdin* means anything at all, it means a formal notice to quit, with a threat of sticks uplifted on the day when I shall have the audacity to repeat the offence.

I believe that the critics have, this time, really over-shot the mark. They struck too hard to strike home. I speak of the critics as a whole, for immersed in the thankless trade of criticism are poets and writers of talent, who have had the good grace to hold out to me the hand of friendship in the midst of the scuffle. I thank them for it. My other judges had all brought out their holiday cudgels. Passion in no way offends me, I quite approve of literary fisticuffs. Only, what fills me with deepest stupefaction, is the absolute innocence of these gentlemen in the face of my work and of my personality. Place them before a Mohican or a Laplander, bringing some barbaric plaything from his country : they could not open more ignorant eyes, nor utter more extraordinary verdicts upon the plaything's mechanism. Not one of them seems to have suspected for an instant that in *The Heirs of Rabourdin* I made a dramatic experiment of a particular kind. They did not even endeavour to account to themselves for the fact that my play is what it is, and not what they

would have wished it to be.   The upshot is, that
they went so far as to discover that I had imitated
everybody.   But there they stopped short, without
asking themselves what reasons could have infatuated
me into imitating everybody.   Did they really think
me simple enough, and dunce enough, not to know
what subject I was selecting?   Am I in the habit o
plundering my colleagues?   Am I unknown?   Am
I a yesterday novice?   And should not the frankness
of my loans from Molière, and from another comic
poet whom I will name later on, have put the critics
on their guard?   The play is what I intended it to
be, let them be sure of that.   Bad or good work, it
matters little; but deliberate work, before all things.

Since the critics have, voluntarily or involuntarily,
passed *The Heirs of Rabourdin* by without discussing
the point of view that I took up, I am reduced to
explaining here what it was that I set myself to do.
Indeed, I should have a good case if I merely wished
to defend myself for having taken as my subject the
eternal cupidity of mankind, the comedy of a group
of heirs awaiting the opening of a will.   In every
literature, at every period, by every humorist, this
comedy has been, is, and will be written.   I have but
continued a tradition which many another will continue after me.   And is not the drama of adultery
equally worn out?   And are there not writers who
live exclusively on this drama, studied in all its
aspects, without being remotely subject to the
reproach of poverty of invention?

But I have no need of this argument.   I confess
that my very settled intention was to write a *pasticcio*
—I mean a special *pasticcio*, written with a certain

idea of experiment.   I proposed, in one word, to go
back to the fountain-head of our stage, to resuscitate
the old literary farce in the form in which our authors
of the sixteenth century borrowed it from the Italians.
So that none might be ignorant of my meaning, I
took from Molière turns of phrases, slices of scenes.
I kept watch upon myself as I wrote each line, so
that my play might remain simple, primitive—naïve
even, if you like.   An intrigue as tenuous as a thread ;
none of the stage effects fashionable in our days ;
sketches of character ; a situation that developed
itself with its side-events until the ultimate catastrophe was reached ; and this catastrophe brought on
by the sheer logic of the facts, without expedients of
any sort.   The only modernisation that I allowed
myself was to dress the characters like ourselves, and
to place them in our own surroundings.   I meant to
make contemporary realism out of the human realism
of all time.

I insist on this starting-point.   There is not a
scene, I repeat, in the play, that ought not to have
opened the critics' eyes, and led them to suspect that
they had before them a protest against the fashion in
which our writers of comedy fritter away Molière's
inheritance.   What has become of that fine laughter,
so simple, so deep in its frankness ; of that living
laughter that has tears in it ?   We have in this age
our comedy of intrigue, a game of patience, a plaything presented to the public.   It has come to be
the accepted model, and it has inflicted upon us a
dramatic code, according to which everything " delays
the action."   You present a character, it " delays the
action ; " you develop a situation, it " delays the

action ; " you give way to a literary caprice, " it delays the action." And the worst is that it has accustomed the public to such complicated stories that the public, in fact, is bored when the stories are not complicated enough. To-day Molière would certainly be recommended to compress *Le Misanthrope* into one act. Again, we have the sentimental comedy, a foolish tear shed between two vaudeville couplets, a bastard breed that delights the sensitive soul. But above all we have the thoughtful comedy, the sermon on the boards, the dramatic art devoted to the amelioration of the race. There we have the triumph of the period. Our authors have abandoned the human side in order to see the social side alone. They study particular social cases, with the result that their plays, after the lapse of ten years, become old-fashioned, and not to be understood of new audiences. They limit themselves to mimic battles with ephemeral prejudices ; they make no pretension towards the absolute ; they seek only for relative truths without experiencing the anguish of those eternal truths that cry aloud in the works of the masters. The masters never preached ; they never sought to prove anything. They lived, and that alone makes of their works lessons for all time.

Such is the case of Molière's inheritance ; and that is why I dreamt of tracing my steps back to that glorious model. I am unworthy, I know. My experiment has, if you like, no worth besides that of having been attempted. None the less, it is worthy, I think, of the esteem of the critics. I had hoped for an analysis that should be, if not sympathetic, at least serious and polite. And I have told with what rudeness the critics hurled themselves upon me and upon my play. Now, it is easy to imagine what my stupor must have been.

Moreover, many of my personal friends doubted whether to applaud me. A farce ! I had written a farce ! Well, yes ! a farce—why not ? I feel in no way compromised, I assure you. The pickle-herring's platform is wider and more epic than our wretched stages on which life is suffocated. The open-air platform, the platform open to the skies, with a frank farce, a farce violently overloaded, a farce that would lend a laugh to the ugly grimace of humanity, permitting itself every licence, " humbugging " death ! That was my dream. I would have liked my farce to be played in a public place, a canvas tent, with a trombone and a big drum at the door. I saw it played by mountebanks, amid somersaults, amid the uproar of a crowd holding its sides. Then, perhaps, it would have been understood. I should not have been insulted by its comparison to a vaudeville. Is not the farce infinite ? It is the unbounded freedom of satire. Beneath the mask distorted by laughter humanity is seen to weep. And therefore the farce has always tempted the men with the broad shoulders : Aristophanes, Shakspeare, Rabelais, Molière. These were buffoons.

I am well aware that our generation would hiss these men of genius, if one fine evening they were to put in an appearance on the Parisian stage. Were Molière to-morrow to produce *Le Malade Imaginaire* or *Georges Dandin*, he would be spat upon by all the critics. They would reproach him with having put nothing but linseed-tea into the first of these masterpieces, and with having portrayed none but rogues and she-rogues in the second. Even recently the fashionable audience of the Comédie-Française were almost revolted at a revival of *Georges Dandin*. All their respect for tradition is wanted to make them accept that superb laughter that knows no fear of anything. It is impossible to play Molière in the provinces. I know of provincial bailiffs and solicitors who, when they come to spend the summer in Paris, take care to consult the placards before taking their wives to the Comédie-Française, lest these ladies should come into contact with the author of *Tartufe*. Molière remains a suspicious character. And what exasperates me in all this is the hypocritical respect borne for the masters. Oh, the masters! there is no one like the masters! copy the masters! But take it into your head one day to listen to this advice, make an experiment, and you shall see what they will do for you. The fact is that the masters scare them. A young man arrives in Paris ; he dreams of acquiring renown as a playwright ; he knocks at the door of one of our most conscientious critics, and he says to him, "I am full of willing-ness. Point out to me those plays I ought to study ; I will set to work to-morrow." You would think, maybe, that the critic will reply, " Study the plays of Molière." Ah, no doubt! He will say, convinced that he is giving excellent and practical advice, " Study the plays of Scribe." That is what we have come to.

I would not wish to mix my personal quarrel with the reflections inspired by the present state of the theatre. I understand, most assuredly, that it is

necessary that we should have plays for the multitude ; nor do I deny the injustice of showing oneself
severe towards men who consent to manufacture
from day to day the so many dozen plays that Paris
needs to fill up its winter.   This comes in the cate-
gory of what is known as Parisian goods.   You cut
out, glue together, sew up, and varnish over : and
there you have a charming gewgaw that lasts you
through a season.   To piece together these plays
a workshop is necessary.   It is essential to have a
general manager, to acquire the ins and outs of the
trade, to know what pleases your customers.   This
attained, there is a whole manual for you to consult.
You must know your Scribe by heart.   He will
teach you in what proportion love may enter into a
comedy ; how much villainy may safely be admitted ;
how to unravel a catastrophe, and how to modify a
character with one wave of the wand.   He will teach
you, in a word, that theatrical "trade" which Molière
knew nothing of, but which the critics of to-day declare to be essential if you aim at rousing the laughter
or the tears of your contemporaries.   All this is
perfectly useful, I grant you.   The public, in fact,
cannot endure any but the most easily digested plays.
It rejects everything that does not issue from the
workshop I spoke of above.   But there are honest
fellows who cannot tie themselves down to the task
of working in stereotyped moulds.   These are mad
enough to contemplate personal works ; they do not
manufacture for a fashion, they endeavour to create
for the ages.   Their presumption is great, no doubt :
no doubt, too, they will never succeed in satisfying
themselves.   Only, I consider them worthy of respect,

and I think that form of criticism obnoxious that makes merry over their fall, and has the malicious intention to condemn them to labour at the pro-duction of the ordinary commercial article.

And see the want of logic in the reproaches cast at me, in the matter of *The Heirs of Rabourdin.* If certain critics are to be credited, mine is a disordered mind that refuses to acknowledge any rule ; my dream is to burn the *Works of Scribe ;* I openly despise the conventions ; I am ripening I know not what project of a theatre of abominations. On the other hand, there are critics who accuse me of being up to the neck in convention, of being two hundred years behind my time in the theatrical movement, of having brought to life the old worm-eaten comedy. And these latter very nearly grasped what it was that I desired to do. What conclusions can be drawn in the face of two statements so opposed to one another? First, that the critics do not always agree among themselves ; next, that if I am a revolutionary when in the presence of idiotic works, I bow with the deepest respect before the works of the masters. I love the masters, as we must needs love them, for their truth. I love them to the extent of desiring to go straight back to them, stepping over the heads of the dwarfs whose capers amuse the crowd. In this matter I reject the relative of talent, and accept only the absolute of genius.

I am not writing this preface in defence of my work. If there is any vigour in it, it will defend itself unaided later on. Nor shall I seek to reply point for point to the violence which it has raised up. I have but one preoccupation: to analyse my case, so that I may draw a moral from it, if possible, for the young writer who may try, as I have done, the effect of truthfulness on the stage. Among the reproaches addressed to me are three which will be sufficient to characterise the general spirit with which I have come into collision. These three reproaches are : my comedy lacks gaiety ; it contains not one sympathetic character ; the situation remains unchanged throughout the three acts. I admit that these are three serious defects from the modern dramatic point of view. It is evident that, if the play be compared, as has been done, with certain contemporary vaudevilles, it will be found to be naïve, too simple and too coarse at the same time. But I do not accept this comparison. I repeat once again, I had other ends in view. I deny that there is any gaiety in Molière—I mean gaiety such as is in demand to-day. Dandin on his knees before his wife makes the heart bleed ; Arnolphe's little attentions to Agnès bring tears of pity to the eyes ; Alceste disquiets one, and Scapin inspires fear. There is a terrible undercurrent to all this laughter. I deny also that Molière ever put himself out to temper the cruelty of his analysis by peopling his plays with sympathetic characters ; apart from his eternal two lovers, who are a concession to the fashion of the day, all the types that he has created are human ; that is to say, rather bad than good. In *L'Avare* they cheat and rob one another from one end to the other. In *Le Misanthrope* all the characters are dubious, so much so that the discussion is to this day continued as to who is the veritable honest man of the play. I pass by the farces, which contain none but fools and

bullies. And lastly I deny that Molière ever suspected a need for complicating a comedy in order to
make it more interesting ; his dramatic work has the
bare precision of a master ; a single course of events
is broadly, logically developed, and gathers to itself
the whole human interest of whatever comes in its
way. I am well aware that in our day the writers
of vaudevilles declare that Molière knew nothing
of playwriting. They might push their frankness
further, and confess flatly that Molière is sad, dread-
ful, and tiresome. They would be telling the sheer
truth.

It will be said that we are no longer in the
seventeenth century, that our civilisation has become
more intricate, and that the drama of to-day cannot
employ the same formula as that of two hundred
years ago. That is quite beyond doubt. There is
no question of imitation. It is simply a question of
going back to the first source of French comic genius.
What we should resuscitate are the broadly-drawn
sketches of character in which the masters of our
stage involved the dominant interest of their works.
Let us copy their fine disdain for ingenious plots ;
let us endeavour to create, as they did, living men,
types of eternal truthfulness. And let us continue to
abide in the realities of to-day, with our own manners,
costume, and surroundings. There, assuredly, is a
formula worth the finding. To my mind that would
be the naturalistic formula that I pointed out in my
preface to *Thérèse Raquin.* I grant that the problem
is no easy one. It is because the formula has not
yet come to me that I thought, in the meanwhile, of
attempting an imitation, *The Heirs of Rabourdin,* in

the hope that the intercourse with the masters would place me on the right road. For me my comedy is but a study, an experiment. With the exception of an occasional portion of a scene, it is outside the formula which I seek.

The time has now come to say from where I took *The Heirs of Rabourdin*. The critics, who have the répertoires of the minor theatres at their fingers' ends, have flung vaudevilles in my face by handfuls. They unearthed astounding instances, whose very titles were unknown to me ; I confess I am grossly ignorant on this subject. I quite simply took the original idea for my play from *Volpone*, a comedy by Ben Jonson, a contemporary of Shakspeare. Not one of the critics thought of this. It is true that the thing called for some little erudition, some interest in foreign literature. Now that I have pointed out the source, I recommend the conscientious critics to read *Volpone*. They will there see what a comedy could be at the time of the English renaissance. I know of no drama more extensive in its audacity. It is a glorious crudeness, a sustained outburst of truth, an admirable paroxysm of satire. Imagine the human beast let loose, with all its appetites. And when one thinks of the audiences that applauded that tremendous laughter ! In sooth, they had nothing in common, neither nerves nor muscles, with our little white-gloved cits, who come to digest at their ease in an orchestra-stall. You can readily believe that I expurgated Ben Jonson. My comedy, to describe which every expression of disgust has been exhausted, is a mere skit by the side of *Volpone*. There is more particularly in the latter a scene, fine to a pitch of terror, which I note for the delicate: one of the heirs comes and offers his wife, his own wife, to the sham dying man, the doctors having decided that a buxom woman was necessary to cure the disease. No literature can produce such a slap in the face for the passions. We are bound of course to accept the refinements of our age; but what artist has not experienced a regret at the thought of those fine, free, and candid centuries, which witnessed the growth of all the hardy annuals of the mind?

It remains for me to insist upon my position as a novelist. When the dramatic critics have said of a new playwright that he is a novelist, they have said everything. This phrase, coming from their pens, means that the novelists are incapable of writing for the stage. I look upon this disdain on the part of the critics as singular. The novelists have made the literary glory of this century. When one of them is willing to apply his talents to the stage, the critics should have nothing for him but encouragement. Certainly, if the stage shed a great lustre on our epoch, if the plays performed were masterpieces, if the dramatic authors bestowed upon the art which they represent all the splendour that could be desired, if, in short, there were no room for a renaissance, then I could understand that we should be repulsed. But the boards are empty; and, whatever might be our failures, they could never equal those of the professional playwrights! We could not possibly bring the stage to a lower level than it is at present. Then why not authorise all our attempts? What we are striving for, in short,

is the enlargement of art.   We try to bring new
blood to bear on it, correctness of diction, a care for
truth.   The novelists, who are the literary princes
of the period, honour our degraded stage, when they
deign to set foot on it.

I repeat, my case is not an isolated one.   I am
pleading now for a whole group of writers.   I am
not so vain as to believe that my slender personality
has alone been sufficient to arouse so much anger.
I am a scapegoat, nothing more.   In me a formula,
rather than a man, has been assailed.   The critics see
expanding before them a group of men who struggle
hard, and will end by making room for themselves.
They don't want the group ; they deny its existence ;
for they would be lost men on the day when they
acknowledged talent.   They would have to accept
the idea of truth that it brings with it, and this would
compel them to change their criterion.   It is not my
play, I say once more, that has been gibbeted ; it is the
naturalistic formula on which it appears to be based.
And I require no further proof of the bias of the
critics than the reports of the first performance.   Not
one of the critics admitted that *The Heirs of
Rabourdin* had been vigorously applauded.*   In this
connection let me quote an acute observation that
an illustrious writer made to me as we left the theatre.
He pressed my hand, and added, as his tribute

---

* In an anti-puff preliminary in the *Star* newspaper a
writer of paragraphs went so far as to assert that at the first
performance in Paris *Les Héritiers Rabourdin* was greeted with
hoots and hisses.   To the imagination of this fantastic person
I in a great measure ascribe the reception accorded to the
production at the Opéra Comique.—A. T.

of appreciation, "To-morrow you will be a great novelist." And indeed, on the next day, the people who have denied me, for ten years, the possession of any talent were exalting my novels in order the better to pummel my play. I will add to this another phrase, a terrible phrase, uttered by an impenitent romanticist, who commands a largely circulating publication which he has made into a political and literary counting-house. He laid down the doctrine of his dramatic theories, and marked me out for his thunderbolts by observing calmly, in a loud voice, without ceremony, "He is too talented ; he is dangerous ; we must keep him down." Nothing that I put into my play is more abominably crude, more satirical of human villainy.

For the rest, what mattered success ? Never has success been in so small a degree a proof of the merit of work as to-day. One thing alone touched me. One Sunday evening I went and sat right in the middle of the house, filled with an unlettered holiday audience. The Saint-Jacques quarter was well represented. The three acts were nothing but one long outburst of laughter. Every word was underlined, nothing escaped that great baby of an audience for whose enjoyment the play, primitive and intentionally naïve, seemed to have been written. They were enchanted with the suggestion of overcolouring; the simplicity of the treatment placed them on an equal footing with the characters of the play. Shall I tell you? I revelled then in the first proud hour of my life.

    *   *   *   *   *

And that is the end of the adventure. A dramatic author, who knows his audiences thoroughly, said to

me : " Think yourself lucky that your play was heard
to the end. Five years ago, no audience would have
consented to listen to so many truths at a time."
And I think myself very lucky if I have indeed
brought about a development in the patience of
audiences. I only wish still to reply to a critic, one
otherwise most sympathetic, who, speaking of *Thérèse
Raquin* and *The Heirs of Rabourdin*, concluded by
saying that this last play was a step backwards ; and
I reply that, at my age, at the stage of work that I
have reached, there are no steps backwards : there
are only steps in every direction, tentative steps to
the right, to the left, wherever it may be interesting
to go.

And now let me make a big parcel of all the
articles that have appeared on *The Heirs of Rabourdin*.
Let me tie up the parcel with string, and carry it up
to my lumber-room. I should not care to make any
capital out of this parcel of insults. Later on it may
be interesting to excavate it. For the moment I
prefer to wash my hands of it. I am accustomed to
expecting no immediate reward for my labours. For
ten years I have been publishing novels, which I fling
behind me, paying no attention to the noise they
make as they fall among the crowd. When there is
a heap of them, the passers-by will be compelled to
take note of them in spite of themselves. I recognise,
now, that the conflict is an identical one in the drama.
My play is scotched, repudiated, drowned amid the
racket of current criticism. What matter? Let me
push my bolts, and exile myself anew in my work.

EMILE ZOLA.

December 1st, 1874.

The
Translator's Note.

❦

THE *Observer*, in its notice of *The Heirs of Rabourdin*, states that mine is "a modified translation;" the *Globe*, that my translation is "exact in the main;" the *Daily Telegraph* thinks that I, "being an experienced playgoer," might have been "given a free hand—not to adapt, but to curtail. No French play, be it tragedy, drama, comedy, or farce, will bear a literal translation, line for line, and word for word." Here, surely, is a divergence of observation as quaint as that of the Parisian critics.

I wish to say in reply to the *Observer*, that my translation was in no way modified; in reply to the *Globe*, that my translation is exact not only in the main, but in every particular; and, in reply to the *Daily Telegraph*, that I was given a free hand, exercised my right of choice, and elected, being an experienced playgoer, to make a literal translation.

A. TEIXEIRA DE MATTOS.

THE TEMPLE, *March 8th*, 1894.

OPERA COMIQUE.
STRAND, W.C.

THE INDEPENDENT THEATRE.
FOUNDER AND SOLE DIRECTOR, J. T. GREIN.

THIRD SEASON, SIXTEENTH PERFORMANCE.

FRIDAY, 23rd February, 1894.

THE
HEIRS OF RABOURDIN,

A COMEDY IN THREE ACTS, BY

EMILE ZOLA.

TRANSLATED BY A. TEIXEIRA DE MATTOS.

DRAMATIS PERSONÆ.

Rabourdin . . .	Mr. JAMES WELCH.
Chapuzot	Mr. HARDING COX.
Dominique . . .	Mr. C. M. HALLARD.
Ledoux	Mr. DOUGLAS GORDON.
Dr. Mourgue . .	Mr. CHARLES GOODHART.
Isaac	Mr. F. NORREYS CONNELL.
Madame Vaussard .	Mrs. ARTHUR AYERS.
Madame Fiquet .	Mrs. LOIS ROYD.
Eugénie	Miss LENA DENE.
Charlotte . . .	Miss MARY JOCELYN.

The Play produced under the direction of
Mr. H. DE LANGE.

The ACTION of the Play takes place at Senlis, at the PRESENT DAY.

Acts I. and III.   In Rabourdin's sitting-room.
Act II.   In Rabourdin's bedroom.

The
Heirs of Rabourdin.

Act I.

*The dining-room of a middle-class house in a
small town. A garden enclosed in walls is seen
at the back through a large glazed door. In the
corner,* L, *there is a porcelain stove, by the side of
which is placed a small occasional table. In the
middle of the wall,* R, *is a sideboard with shelves.*
L U E *is a door leading into Rabourdin's bedroom.*
L, *down stage, is a safe let into the wall.* R U E
*is a door leading into the kitchen. There is a
round table in the middle of the stage, with an
arm-chair fronting the audience behind the table.*
L *is a chair, and* R *is a wicker-work sofa, with
two tapestried cushions. Near the safe is a little
flower-stand; a barometer hangs beside the sideboard. On the sideboard is a liqueur-stand, a
tray, a goblet, cups, etc. There are several chairs:
one is in marqueterie and stands near the stove. A*

I

cuckoo-clock hangs on wall R, *down stage. It is ten o'clock on a spring morning.*

SCENE I.

CHARLOTTE,   RABOURDIN.

Rabourdin.

You are sure, then, Charlotte, that the safe is empty?

Charlotte.

(*looking into the safe*) Empty, godfather, quite empty. (*Crosses* R, *while Rabourdin looks into the safe.*)

Rabourdin.

That's strange.

Charlotte.

What? Strange that there should be no more money? (*Laughing*) You are quite funny, god-father! There is not often money in the safe. (*They both come down stage.*)

Rabourdin.

It is no laughing matter, Charlotte. It is abso-lutely necessary that I should pay that jew Isaac his old bill for that Louis Treize press he sold me.

Charlotte.

He'll wait. He need not be frightened about his money, I should think. I could bring you back the whole of Senlis in my basket when I go out, if I wished to. I should think so! Why, you're Old Daddy Moneybags! Monsieur Rabourdin, who used to keep the draper's shop on the market-place, at the sign of "Le Grand Saint Martin." Why, he

must have saved ten thousand francs a year at least!
The good people! they little think the safe is empty.

Rabourdin.

(*startled, looking behind him*) Hush, chatterbox!
(*Confidingly*) My nephews and nieces haven't seemed
so affectionate the last few days.

Charlotte.

That's serious.

Rabourdin.

They would let me die like a dog, mind you.
That lot, whom I've fed for ten years, and who
have stripped me of my last sou!

Charlotte.

Well, they're giving it you back now. You'll
soon be quits. Be fair, godfather, they're decent
enough, your heirs. They're fighting for your
legacy with presents, big and small. You're in
clover, you are—tucked-in, kissed, tickled, and
worshipped.

Rabourdin.

The rascals! They've taken all I've got, and
they want what's left! If I hadn't played the
miser when I had hardly a farthing left, I shouldn't
have had a crust of bread or a glass of water from
them. Ah! if they only knew, there would be no
more dainties, my poor Charlotte; no more petting,
no more serene old age for me! I should be "that
old scamp of a Rabourdin."

Charlotte.

You'll have to find the money for old Isaac in
that case.

Rabourdin.

Find the money ?   I like that !   Where the devil do you expect me to find it ?   If I borrow it, all Senlis will know.   My poor house is crushed under mortgages as it is.

Charlotte.

Well, there are your heirs.

Rabourdin.

What ! do you think I might?   They've given me a lot lately.   Well, let's see how we stand. Take the ledger.   (*Charlotte crosses L and takes out the ledger from the safe, while Rabourdin goes up to the table, and sits down at it in the arm-chair, which he has drawn towards him.*)   I might perhaps get twenty francs from one, and twenty from another. The great thing is not to squeeze them dry.

Charlotte.

(*brings up a chair from L and sits down on it, facing Rabourdin*)   What you've had since the first, eh, godfather ?

Rabourdin.

Yes.

Charlotte.

(*opening ledger on the table*)   Let me see.   (*Reading*) " Boucharain, on the second, a little parcel containing twelve pairs of socks, six cakes of soap, a pair of razors, four scarves, and three yards of cloth for a frock-coat."

Rabourdin.

Good, good !   There's no one like these general agents.   I'll spare that one.   Go on.

Charlotte.

(*reading*) " The widow Guérard, on the seventh, a leg of mutton."

Rabourdin.

And—

Charlotte.

And—nothing more !

Rabourdin.

(*springing up*) What, nothing! Is my niece Guérard making a fool of me? A leg of mutton on the seventh, and to-day is the eighteenth ! At that rate I can have as many nieces as I like. To be a niece of Rabourdin's puts you in the Senlis set ! It means expectations to the tune of a hundred thousand francs.

Charlotte.

(*continuing*) " Lehudier, on the ninth———"

Rabourdin.

(*interrupting her*) Oh, skip the tradespeople, and let's get to the legatees who mean business, to those whom I see every day. (*He sits down on the sofa.*)

Charlotte.

(*reading*) " Doctor Mourgue———"

Rabourdin.

(*interrupting*) That dear, good doctor ! There's a man who understands his patients ! And what has he contributed ?

Charlotte.

" Three pots of jam on the seventh, and two quarts of syrup on the thirteenth."

Rabourdin.

Ah, well, but that's nice, that's decent of him, is it not, Charlotte? He's not a relation; one can't expect more than that.

Charlotte.

(*continuing*) "Chapuzot——" (*Interrupting herself*) Your former partner; he is not a member of the family either.

Rabourdin.

(*lowering his voice with a frightened look*) Oh, that one! A coughing old corpse, with a whole string of incurable complaints. Chapuzot is eighty. I am only sixty, thank God! And it's my house he's after; it's my freehold he's been after these thirty years.

Charlotte.

He gave a lot of raspberry bushes for the garden, three pear trees, and some flowers and vegetables for planting.

Rabourdin.

By Jove! he's fixing up his garden, he thinks it's his already.

Charlotte.

(*reading*) "Madame Vaussard——"

Rabourdin.

Oh, that dear old Olympe! What has she given?

Charlotte.

(*reading*) "On the fifth, a silver napkin-ring; on the fifteenth a goblet."

Rabourdin.

That's true, I had forgotten all about that. That's

like my luck. That dear Olympe spends all her
money on her dress. It's no use asking anything
from the husband, a great ass of an architect, who
works himself to death, and never has a sou. And
to think that not long ago I lent them any amount
of money.

Charlotte.

And then there's Madame Fiquet, who gave you
two hundred francs on the sixth.

Rabourdin.

(*rising*) That poor Lisbeth! She is the only one
who knows how to find any money.

Charlotte.

(*rising*) I like that! The widow of a sheriff's
officer! I should like to have all the thousand-franc
notes that she's had out of you!

Rabourdin.

She has too many irons in the fire. But she's
a woman who knows her way about, and who'd
raise a crop of five-franc pieces on the paving stones.
And so that's all, Charlotte? Isn't there a nephew,
or a niece, or any one?

Charlotte.

(*taking the ledger from the table*) There's only
Monsieur Ledoux, the young man who is to marry
your little niece Eugénie. (*Showing the ledger to
Rabourdin*) Ledoux—a bunch of flowers—a bunch
of flowers—and a bunch of flowers.

Rabourdin.

Yes, flowers, nothing but flowers! (*Crossing L*)
So there's nobody! Great Heavens! what am I to

do ? Isaac will come just at breakfast-time, when
they will all be there. I shall be a ruined man if
they suspect the least thing.

Charlotte.

Don't distress yourself like that. How much is
it you want ?

Rabourdin.

Two hundred and seventy-two francs.

Charlotte.

Well, then, take it out of my aunt's three thousand
francs that you hold in trust for me.

Rabourdin.

(*nervously*) Out of your dowry ? Never, never!
I would rather dig the earth with my finger-nails.

Charlotte.

How excited you get! I hope you have not been
playing any of your tricks here, godfather?

Rabourdin.

(*with a forced laugh*) You make me laugh! The
scrip is in a little corner to itself. Do you wish to
see it ? No, do not press me, my mind's made up.
That money is sacred. Never mind, I'll find some
means. Isn't breakfast ready ?

Charlotte.

Yes, I am going to lay the cloth. (*Goes to the
sideboard, and from it takes a tablecloth, which she
lays on the table.*)

Rabourdin.   ·

(*going to the cuckoo clock*, R, *and looking at the time*)
Nearly ten. They will be here soon. (*Turns,
and observes the safe.*) The devil! It's silly to

leave the safe open. (*In passing by the table he takes the ledger from it, and hides it at the bottom of the safe, which he closes and locks, slips the key into his waistcoat pocket, and then comes down stage.*) Two hundred and seventy-two francs! That will be a job. I will go and put on my yellow dressing-gown; it makes me look like a corpse. (*He goes towards the door of his bedroom, l, and comes back to Charlotte.*) Do I look well this morning?

Charlotte.

Wonderfully well.

Rabourdin.

So much the worse. And my eyes?

Charlotte.

Your eyes are in excellent condition. They laugh and sparkle like live coals.

Rabourdin.

Worse and worse. Then I don't look like a man at death's door?

Charlotte.

You! No one would think you were twenty.

Rabourdin.

That's terrible. You feed me too well, Charlotte. I am growing young! I shall be ruined. And I have such an appetite that I feel capable of eating like a wolf in front of them! I shan't get anything, not a sou, not one sou! (*He goes out by door l. Charlotte puts the arm-chair back in its place, and takes back the chair to l. Dominique comes in quietly. He carries a little parcel at the end of a stick, which he lets fall behind the sofa. At the sound Charlotte turns round and throws herself into his arms.*)

SCENE II.

CHARLOTTE,   DOMINIQUE.

Charlotte.

(*with a suppressed cry*) Dominique ! (*They embrace*) You, at Senlis !

Dominique.

(*holding her hands*) Ah, isn't it a fine surprise ? I would not write to you. (*They separate and look at one another, with amazement*) How handsome you've grown, and how big and strong !

Charlotte.

How handsome you've grown, and how big and strong !

Dominique.

Five years since we last saw one another. But I thought of you.

Charlotte.

Yes, five years. And I—I waited for you.

Dominique.

Well, that's all over. I am a man now. I told them that I was going back to the country. And I have come to fetch you, my dear wife. (*During this speech he has given her his arm, and they walk slowly* R, *returning to the middle of the stage while Charlotte is speaking.*)

Charlotte.

My dear husband. Do you remember my Aunt Nanon's mill? The kind old thing, God rest her soul! When I used to come down, all white with flour, I would find you on the bank of the mill-stream.

You would walk three miles to come and help me pull down the magpies' nests. Ah, those rascals of magpies! They were right at the top of the poplar-trees. I used to fasten up my petticoats with string before climbing. I had no fear, I climbed as high as you did ; and we used to say good-day to one another from one tree to the other, right up in the air. And down below, at the bottom of the great pit, the mill went tick-tack.

Dominique.

(*kissing her hand*) Yes, I remember, I remember.

Charlotte.

And the day we went for a ride on La Noiraude, the old mare of the mill. We went along the high road, quite far. When we came to the hill, you remember, you left me alone on La Noiraude, and I began to kick her in the stomach with my heels, and she ran off like a wild beast. You screamed out, you were afraid that she would pitch me into the ditch. And that made me laugh so much that I caught the mare round the neck, so that I might laugh comfortably. It was dark before we heard the tick-tack of the mill at the other end of the meadows. (*Dominique, who has taken her in his arms, kisses her in the neck.*) You remember, you remember !

Dominique.

Yes, you were a scapegrace. Your Aunt Nanon used to cry, "She's a boy, that girl!" And I, I loved you because you used to climb the trees and were not afraid of La Noiraude. You're a fine, buxom woman now.

Charlotte.

You don't look delicate, either.

Dominique.

And how studious you were with all that ! You used to throw stones at me when I tried to make you play truant. If you had only cared to become a young lady, you could have become a young lady with any of them.

Charlotte.

That would have bored me to a certainty. I would rather be your wife. I swore that, to begin with.

Dominique.

Yes, we swore it. We swore to get married, one morning in the sunshine, behind a hedge. When shall it be—now ?

Charlotte.

Oh, at once, as soon as the priest is ready. Aunt Nanon left me three thousand francs when she died. I will ask my godfather to give me my dowry, and then we'll get married.

Dominique.

Three thousand francs ! Why, you're a rich woman, Charlotte ! I felt quite conceited when I came here. But now, I dare not tell you.

Charlotte.

What is it ?

Dominique.

I have saved a little money. Three hundred francs, a poor three hundred francs, scraped together sou by sou. I have it with me, in my pocket.

Charlotte.

My dear Dominique ! That will be for my chain
and my wedding ring. What a lovely day it is, and
how pleasant life is ! (*She takes his arm.*) Listen, this
is my dream. I believe Aunt Nanon's mill is to let.
When we are married we will go and see, we will
put our money into it, and I shall be the happy
miller's wife, all white with flour, as in the days
when I used to find you sitting by the mill-stream.
We will have a mare, and our urchins will pull
down the magpies' nests. Are you willing ? We
shall love each other always, always, to the sound of
the tick-tack of the mill.

Dominique.

(*kissing her again in the neck*) Am I willing ?

Charlotte.

(*escaping from him, and going up to the sideboard*)
Do stop, you prevent me from laying the table.
My godfather's nieces will be here presently.

Dominique.

I'll stay ; so much the worse for them !

Charlotte.

(*coming down stage with a plate, which she wipes*)
The thing is, those gossips chatter. I should have
preferred not to say who you are until later on, when
things are over. (*She puts the plate on the table.*)
There is one way out of it. Listen. When they
are all there, you must come in boldly, and say to
my godfather, who has never seen you, " Good-day,
uncle."

Dominique.

But he is not my uncle.

Charlotte.

That makes no difference.

Dominique.

He will ask me where I come from, who my
father is, and what I have come to Senlis for.

Charlotte.

If he asks that, tell him whatever you like: the
first thing that comes into your head.

Dominique.

And will that story satisfy him ?

Charlotte.

Perfectly.   Quick, go to the kitchen, and come
back in a few minutes.   Here come the troop of
them.   (*She lets him out by the door* R, *and goes on
laying the table.   The heirs enter one after the other.*)

SCENE III.

CHARLOTTE, CHAPUZOT, DOCTOR MOURGUE, then
     MADAME VAUSSARD, MADAME FIQUET,
     EUGÉNIE, LEDOUX.

Chapuzot.

(*entering on the arm of the doctor, and coming down the
stage* R)   So the small-pox is claiming many victims
in Senlis, doctor?

Mourgue.

Out of thirty patients, I have twenty infected by
the epidemic.

Chapuzot.

That's a fine number.   And what is the proportion
of fatal cases ?

Mourgue.

Fifteen out of twenty, I should say. Have you been vaccinated, Chapuzot?

Chapuzot.

Not I. I don't need that. They tried to vaccinate me. It wouldn't take—I am too strong. (*He is seized with a fit of coughing which throws him back on the sofa.*)

Mourgue.

You ought to look after that cough of yours.

Chapuzot.

(*rising furiously*) I am not coughing. I have something in my throat. I never swallowed a drug in my life, doctor, and here I am, and sound too! I'll outlive you all. Hee-hee! (*He crosses* L) I've seen a good few off as it is. Senlis is being cleared out.

Mourgue.

Pooh! You'll die like the rest, my friend. People die from a mere nothing, without thinking about it.

Chapuzot.

(*lowering his voice, and pointing to door* L) Hush! Suppose that poor Rabourdin were to hear you!

Charlotte.

He has had a bad night! He got up late, he is dressing. (*She goes into Rabourdin's room,* L.)

Chapuzot.

It's a bad symptom, at his age, when you get up late. However, we must be sensible about it. (*He sits down on chair* L) He would be much happier if he were dead.

Mourgue.

(*who has gone up stage, near the door, to place his hat on a chair*) Ah! here is the beautiful Madame Vaussard.

Madame Vaussard.

(*entering*) Always gallant, doctor. (*She takes off her hat, and hangs it up near the stove.*)

Mourgue.

And you, Madame, are always young, always elegant, the Queen of Senlis! (*Kisses her hand.*) And how is our excellent Monsieur Vaussard?

Madame Vaussard.

Thanks, he is at home, he is working. (*Coming down stage*) I herald the coming of my cousin Fiquet with her boarding-school.

Mourgue.

How do you mean, her boarding-school?

Madame Vaussard.

(*laughing, crossing* R) Why, her daughter Eugénie and young Ledoux. (*The doctor sits down on the sofa, takes a newspaper from his pocket, and reads it attentively.*)

Madame Fiquet.

(*enters briskly with a basket on her arm, and takes off her bonnet and shawl, which she places on a chair near the sideboard.*) Well! and hasn't our uncle begun his breakfast yet?

Chapuzot.

It seems that Rabourdin has not had a wink of sleep all night.

Madame Fiquet.

(*coming down stage*) It must be his gout. (*Places*

her basket on the table, and goes up to Madame Vaussard.) I beg your pardon, cousin: good-morning. I am quite out of sorts.   I have been running about all the morning for one of my friends; it's a divorce-case in which I am interesting myself a little: the poor woman is almost off her head.   I have all the documents in my basket.   That's a pretty dress you have on, cousin.   What did you pay for it ?

Madame Vaussard.
The material ?   I don't know exactly.

Madame Fiquet.
I should have liked to make a comparison.   I have some patterns of stuff here.   (*Shewing her basket*)   It's a bankrupt stock.   I am selling dress-lengths, just to oblige them.   (*Sits down in the arm-chair, behind the table.*)   Ah, my dear friends, if you knew how difficult it is to carry the most trifling bit of business through !

Madame Vaussard.
(*sitting down on a chair by the sofa*)   And shan't I be able to give a kiss to my dear Eugénie ?

Madame Fiquet.
(*surprised*)   What, Eugénie?

Madame Vaussard.
Yes, your daughter; I thought she was with you.

Madame Fiquet.
My daughter?   That's true, she was with me. (*rising and calling out*)   Minette ! Minette !

Eugénie.
(*enters with Ledoux.*)   Here we are, mamma.   We were in the arbour, enjoying the breeze.   Good

morning, aunt. (*Comes down stage, and kisses Madame Vaussard, who has risen from her chair.*)

Chapuzot.

(*to Ledoux, who has come and shaken hands with him*) Ah! youth, youth! You should be more careful.

Ledoux.

I am quite well, I assure you.

Chapuzot.

You never know, you never know.

Madame Fiquet.

Come, children, go back to the garden, and pick a nosegay for your uncle. · (*Eugénie and Ledoux go out. Madame Fiquet and Madame Vaussard sit down again, one in the arm-chair, the other on the chair.*)

SCENE IV.

MADAME FIQUET, MADAME VAUSSARD,
MOURGUE, CHAPUZOT.

Mourgue.

(*still on the sofa, reading his paper*)   I see Turks are down one franc.

Madame Fiquet.

I believe our uncle has some money invested in that stock.

Madame Vaussard.

Monsieur Chapuzot, do you know if our uncle has any Turkish bonds?

Chapuzot.

Yes, he is sure to have some. (*Rises and takes the centre of the stage*)   Rabourdin has never been lucky with his investments. He is not clever. (*The women both rise, seized with anxiety.*)

Madame Vaussard.
He has made a nice little fortune, nevertheless.

Chapuzot.
Certainly, I don't say not.

Madame Vaussard.
One of the handsomest fortunes in Senlis.

Chapuzot.
Yes, yes.

Madame Fiquet.
Why do you shake your head ? Say what you mean. Has he lost it all ?

Chapuzot.
No, no, he's not clever, that's all ! When we were in business together he used to drive me to despair. I don't know where the firm would have been without me. There would have been no business done at all. I made all the money. Ah, Rabourdin is very much indebted to me. (*Goes up stage and crosses* L.) Why, it's like that safe. Do you see, it's not in its right place ? He only kept it and had it built in there to annoy me.

Madame Vaussard.
(*coming up to the safe*) It looks a respectable safe, that.

Madame Fiquet.
(*examining the lock*) It's a good make.

Madame Vaussard.
(*laughing*) What should you say there was inside ?

I'll bet it is all in five-franc pieces. (*Goes up stage, and sits down in the arm-chair.*)

Madame Fiquet.

Pooh! our uncle is quite right to like money, and the safe looks very well there. (*Taps on the safe.*) It's a good safe, a lucky safe, a faithful safe.

Chapuzot.

(*who has remained up stage, grinning, walking up and down with short steps*) As to the enjoyment that Rabourdin is able to get out of his money now —what do you say, doctor?

Mourgue.

(*without raising his head from his paper*) Yes!

Madame Fiquet.

I was afraid some loss might have upset him. (*She rummages in her basket, takes a little packet out of it, and goes towards the kitchen* R.) Ah! I was forgetting, I have brought him some digestive food. I will go and make him some gruel of it. It is very strengthening, and delicious to taste. (*On the threshold of the door, turning back*) You ought to eat a little plateful of it every morning, cousin, you who like keeping a clear complexion.

SCENE V.

CHAPUZOT, MADAME VAUSSARD, MOURGUE.

Madame Vaussard.

(*rising brusquely, and watching Madame Fiquet go out*) That artful woman! She won't be happy until she takes to washing up the crockery in this house!

Chapuzot.

(*still up stage, sniffing about*) Hee, hee!

Madame Vaussard.

(*crossing* R) She would choke our uncle with her gruel, if she could. Besides, a milk diet is no good for old men. Isn't that so, doctor?

Mourgue.

(*still reading his paper*) Yes.

Madame Vaussard.

(*crossing* L) A woman of no position, who makes her living nobody knows how. Always shabbily dressed, her hair all tangled, and her face hardly washed.

Chapuzot.

(*who has come down to the table* R) The good lady carries an inexhaustible basket. (*Lifting the basket*) The devil! It's no light weight! (*Rummaging in the basket*) Pots of pomade, protested bills, samples of wine.

Madame Vaussard.

(*taking up the rummaging*) Photographs, a dentist's prospectus, a parcel of old lace, a bundle of letters done up in pink tape, an address of a midwife, a gold bracelet.

Chapuzot.

(*continuing*) And a specimen of the indiarubber corset of which she has been talking all the last week. She could open a bazaar. (*Crosses* L.)

Madame Vaussard.

It's a disgrace! If one only chose to talk! (*To Chapuzot*) See here, it was she who set the school-

master against his wife. (*To Mourgue*)   And then
it was she again who married that poor Mademoiselle
Reverchon to that brute of an apothecary, whom
she was obliged to leave within a week. (*To both
Chapuzot and Mourgue*)   She would throw Senlis
into a turmoil if she were allowed to have her way.
She will never benefit by our uncle's will, in spite of
the baseness of her flattery.

Chapuzot.

I believe, on the contrary, that he will leave her
everything. She is reckoning on that in order to
marry her daughter. The little one is much run
after.

Madame Vaussard.

What nonsense !   Our uncle would never be such
a fool. Don't you think so, doctor ?

Mourgue.

(*still absorbed in his paper*)   Yes. (*Chapuzot returns
to his chair,* L, *grinning, and sits down.*)

Madame Vaussard.

Ah, everybody is not like me !   I am too proud
for that. I keep my station. You will never see
me going down on my knees. I would rather not
receive the least remembrance of my uncle than
lower myself to one of those self-interested services
which degrade the hand that performs them.

Madame Fiquet.

(*returning, and taking a plate from the sideboard*)
And now I am going to gather some strawberries.

Madame Vaussard.

(*running up quickly, and snatching the plate from her*)
Don't trouble, I'll pick the strawberries ! (*Goes out* C.)

SCENE VI.

CHAPUZOT, MADAME FIQUET, MOURGUE.

Madame Fiquet.

(*thunderstruck, following Madame Vaussard with her eyes*) Eh! What does she mean? Can't I pick strawberries as well as she? The artful woman! (*Comes down stage.*)

Chapuzot.

(*grinning*) Damme, she's making herself useful!

Madame Fiquet.

A respectable woman who plays all kinds of tricks on her great booby of a husband! The beautiful Madame Vaussard! She is thirty-five, and is as matured as an over-ripe pear.

Chapuzot.

(*rising, and coming toward her*) No, be fair, she is very nice-looking still, and just the build that pleases a man.

Madame Fiquet.

A man! You should have said the whole town. Everybody knows of it. She has young men in each of her cupboards. I tell you she wears false hair and paints her face! Isn't it true, doctor, she paints her face?

Mourgue.

(*still reading his paper*) Yes, yes, she paints her face.

Madame Fiquet.

And you give her hints about face-washes and pomades?

Mourgue.
Yes, just so, face-washes and pomades.

Madame Fiquet.
Besides, those dresses she wears always give her a look of I don't know what. They must cost her a good deal, her dresses! So much the better, so much the better : we shall see what sort of end the beautiful Madame Vaussard will come to! Ah, madame gives dinner-parties, lives as well as the sous-préfet, wears a new dress every week, has nice young men to tea! That's right! The day will come when she won't have bread to eat.

Chapuzot.
Unless Rabourdin leaves her his money.

Madame Fiquet.
You're jesting.

Chapuzot.
Not a bit. Her creditors show patience. She has all the credit she wants. She need only mention her uncle's name to find a lender.

Madame Fiquet.
That's just it—pure swindling! She has all sorts of shady transactions with that usurer of an Isaac, the furniture-dealer, who lends out money by the week, and who beats the country-side to pick up antiquities. Come, come, the beautiful Madame Vaussard does not make me at all uneasy.

Chapuzot.
Just as you please. If you refuse to see things as they are.

Madame Fiquet.
You know something then ?

Chapuzot.

What! haven't you guessed that she wants to prevent the marriage of your daughter with Monsieur Ledoux? She was on particularly good terms with Monsieur Ledoux last winter. She used to stuff him with cakes in her dressing-room.

Madame Fiquet.

If I thought that were true!

Chapuzot.

(*going up stage*) It's so true, that there she is at this moment picking strawberries with the young man.

Madame Fiquet.

(*going up stage*) Thank you, Monsieur Chapuzot. To take away Monsieur Ledoux from my poor Minette! (*Looking into the garden*) I really believe she is making him kiss her hand. Wait, I will go and watch them through the kitchen-window. (*She goes out hurriedly* R.)

SCENE VII.

CHAPUZOT,   MOURGUE.

Mourgue.

(*to Chapuzot, who laughs, as he sits down on the chair* L) You will end by setting them by the ears. (*He folds up his paper and rises.*)

Chapuzot.

Well, it amuses me! They are comical when they are angry. One must laugh a little.

Mourgue.

To sum up, which of them will be the heiress, in your opinion?

Chapuzot.

(*rising*) Which of them? Neither one nor the other! What! do you still believe that Rabourdin would leave his money to those two gossips? He's an ass, but not such an ass as that.

Mourgue.

They are his nieces.

Chapuzot.

A stout woman with the appetite of an ogress, whose pretensions would become unendurable if she had any money in her pocket.

Mourgue.

She is his niece.

Chapuzot.

A shady old hag, who is mixed up in all the dirty transactions of Senlis, and who would swallow up the fortunes of ten people without the chink of a single crown being heard.

Mourgue.

But, damme, she's his niece!

Chapuzot.

(*exasperated, crossing* R) His niece! his niece! what has that to do with it? Who leaves his money to his nieces? (*Lowering his voice*) What is the good of nieces, when Rabourdin is surrounded by devoted friends, friends of his heart, who don't let a single day pass without coming to see him?

Mourgue.

(*confidentially*)   You think then that our poor Rabourdin—?

Chapuzot.

It has all been arranged long ago. Think ! we have known one another forty years. I shall have the house. I expect to take possession in the autumn. (*He is seized with a fit of coughing which throws him back on the sofa.*)

Mourgue.

(*aside*) Yes, when the leaves fall. (*Aloud*) Take care of that cough—do you hear ? It will play you some nasty trick or other.

Chapuzot.

(*rising, in a rage*) Leave off ! Something has only gone the wrong way.

Mourgue.

(*lowering his voice*) Listen ! Between ourselves, I may as well warn you that Madame Fiquet has had a promise from her uncle.

Chapuzot.

A promise ? Does Rabourdin make promises to all the world, then ?

Mourgue.

Damme, he gets himself petted ; he's quite right. The house will go to the kindest, to the most loving one. Be loving, Chapuzot.

Chapuzot.

You're making fun of me ! You don't suppose I am going to stir soups or gather strawberries, do you ? Ah no, doctor ; I have too much self-respect for that. (*Changing his tone little by little*) The fact is that I have never been able to endure the sight of suffering. Rabourdin would have been dead by now, but for me. Look, the table is not even laid! There's no salt, no pepper, no bread, no napkin. (*He removes Madame Fiquet's basket, and finishes laying the cloth.*)

Mourgue.

(*aside, laughing*)   Upon my honour, they're all equally funny!   (*Sits down on chair* L.)   I shan't stir a foot. I have a formal promise from Rabourdin. They won't catch me performing menial offices. (*He observes Charlotte coming in, and taking one of the cushions from the sofa; he rises and snatches it from her hands.*)   Give that here, that is the doctor's duty. You always put it too low down.   (*He arranges the cushions in the arm-chair.*)   There, that will be comfortable.   (*At this moment, Rabourdin appears at the door* L, *bent and broken like a dying man. Mourgue pats the cushion. Chapuzot cuts bread. The other characters enter as follows : Madame Fiquet,* R, *carrying a basin of soup ; Madame Vaussard,* C, *with a plate of strawberries ; Eugénie and Ledoux, also* C, *with nosegays.*)

SCENE VIII.

RABOURDIN, CHARLOTTE, MOURGUE, EUGENIE, MADAME VAUSSARD, LEDOUX, CHAPUZOT, MADAME FIQUET.

All.

Ah ! here he is !

Madame Vaussard and Madame Fiquet.

Our dear uncle !

Chapuzot and Mourgue.
Our dear old friend!

Rabourdin.

Thank you, thank you, my children.

Mourgue.

(*goes to bring him in.*)   There, come and sit down.   I have arranged the cushions, you will be as comfortable as though you were in bed.   (*Presses him into the arm-chair.*)

Madame Fiquet.

(*coming nearer, to the* R *of the table*)   And you will eat your gruel, won't you? semolina with milk and sugar—a real dainty.   I made it for you myself. (*She puts the gruel on the table.*)

Madame Vaussard.

(*coming near, to* L *of the table*)   There, I picked them for you.   They are delicious.   (*She places the straw-berries on the table.*)

Chapuzot.

(*coming near, facing the table*)   I have been cutting you some bread, the crust, from the brown end.

Rabourdin.

Thank you, thank you, my children.

Eugénie.

(*coming down stage with Ledoux, while Madame Vaussard and Madame Fiquet stand a little aside*) Will you allow us to offer you these flowers?

Rabourdin.

(*standing up*) Oh, flowers! (*Utters a cry of pain*) Ah! My back aches!

Mourgue.

(*rushing up, pushing Eugénie and Ledoux aside*)
You tire him. (*To Rabourdin*) I am holding the
cushions, do not be afraid.

Madame Fiquet.

(*supporting him on the left*)   Lean on my arm.

Madame Vaussard.

(*supporting him on the right*)   Gently, gently.

Chapuzot.

(*who has gone up behind the chair*)   Lower him very
slowly, don't shake him.   That's right. (*Rabourdin
sits down.*)

All.

Ah, there he is !

Madame Fiquet and Madame Vaussard.

Our dear uncle !

Chapuzot and Mourgue.

Our dear old friend ! (*Eugénie and Ledoux return
slyly to the garden.   Madame Vaussard hands the
bouquets to Charlotte, who goes and places them on the
stove, and goes out afterwards by door* R.)

SCENE IX.

MADAME VAUSSARD, MOURGUE, RABOURDIN,
MADAME FIQUET, CHAPUZOT.

Rabourdin.

(*seated*)   I breathe again.   My legs feel so heavy.

Mourgue.

Upon my soul, we look very ill this morning.
(*Takes his pulse.*)

Rabourdin.

Don't I, doctor? Very ill indeed. I have spent a horrid night.

Mourgue.

The pulse says nothing. Let us see the tongue. The tongue says nothing either. I don't like this absence of symptoms. That is always very serious.

Rabourdin.

Is it not, doctor?

Mourgue.

I will write you a little prescription. (*Goes up stage and writes the prescription on the occasional table near the stove.*)

Madame Fiquet.

(*standing near Rabourdin*) Pooh! our uncle will live another hundred years.

Chapuzot.

(*sitting on the sofa*) A hundred years is a long time.

Madame Vaussard.

(*sitting on chair* L) The Rabourdins have their lives screwed in to their bodies.

Chapuzot.

(*getting angry, and rising*) What? what nonsense! He knows how ill he is as well as you do. Don't you, Rabourdin?

Rabourdin.

(*in a voice of suffering*) Yes, yes, my friend.

Chapuzot.

And then he is always laid up, always doctoring himself. I think there is something the matter with his blood.

Rabourdin.

(*nervously*) My friend, my dear friend——

Chapuzot.

I am not saying this to frighten you. But there, you're not a strong man. The least thing might carry you off. You know what you're in for, damme !

Rabourdin.

(*growing angry*) I beg your pardon, Chapuzot, I am not dead yet. You're unendurable ! (*Chapuzot returns to the sofa, and sits down again.*)

Madame Fiquet.

Why, our uncle is in wonderful health.

Madame Vaussard.

He will outlive us all yet.

Rabourdin.

(*resuming his suffering voice*) No no; Chapuzot is right, I am very weak. Ah, my poor children, you will not have me among you long.

Mourgue.

(*who has finished writing his prescription, coming down stage*) There. You must take a table-spoonful of the mixture once an hour ; then, after each meal, one of the powders; three of the pills every morning; and besides, an alkali bath every other day. If the pain grows worse, send for me this afternoon. (*Goes and fetches his hat near the door.*)

Rabourdin.

(*raising his voice*) Doctor, I may eat, may I not?

Mourgue.

(*returning*) A little, my friend, a very little. Good-bye. (*He goes out. Madame Vaussard brings her chair up to the table, and begins picking the strawberries. Madame Fiquet ties the napkin round Rabourdin's neck. Chapuzot remains seated on the sofa.*)

SCENE X.

MADAME VAUSSARD, RABOURDIN, MADAME FIQUET, CHAPUZOT, later CHARLOTTE.

Madame Fiquet.
The gruel will get cold. Come, uncle, make an effort.

Chapuzot.
He would do better not to eat. Eh, my poor Rabourdin, you have not much appetite to-day?

Rabourdin.
Ugh! Ugh!

Madame Fiquet.
Only just a spoonful, to please us.

Chapuzot.
(*rising*) Ah no ; leave him alone, if he's not hungry.

Rabourdin.
And yet——

Chapuzot.
His bed is what he wants, that is evident.

Rabourdin.
Excuse me ! I'm not hungry. Only I seem to have—a sort of hollow feeling in my inside. (*Chapuzot sits down.*)

Madame Fiquet.
Yes, yes, make an effort. Eat what you can.

3

Rabourdin.
(*eating*) Just a little, just a little. It's all over, this time. Soon I shan't put you out any more, I shall make room for you.

Madame Vaussard.
Oh, uncle, how can you talk like that? (*Pours him out some wine.*)

Rabourdin.
(*eating gluttonously*) No, don't make a mistake. I feel I am sinking fast.

Chapuzot.
(*rushing up to take away the basin from him*) Rabourdin, you will do yourself harm. I have been watching you. (*Rabourdin pushes him aside, and drinks up the remainder of the gruel.*) Just look, he has emptied the basin. (*He returns to his seat.*)

Madame Fiquet.
That is because he thought my gruel good. There's not a drop left. Now, drink up your glass of wine, and I will call Charlotte to clear away.

Madame Vaussard.
(*rising up quickly, holding the plate of strawberries*) Ah, excuse me, I want my uncle to taste my strawberries.

Madame Fiquet.
(*bitterly*) But he can't choke himself in order to please you.

Madame Vaussard.
(*growing angry*) I let him stuff himself with your gruel, did I not? It is very indigestible, that mess!

You're going to eat my strawberries, are you not, uncle?

Madame Fiquet.

(*pushing at the plate*) We shall see. I will not allow him to be forced to upset himself.

Rabourdin.

Lisbeth, Olympe! I beg of you. (*Madame Vaussard places the strawberries before him.*) I thought that before the strawberries——

Madame Vaussard.

Before the strawberries——

Rabourdin.

Yes, Charlotte had promised me——

Madame Fiquet.

What?

Rabourdin.

A little cutlet.

Chapuzot.

A cutlet! But he'll have indigestion!

Rabourdin.

Oh, quite a little one, only the lean, just to nibble at. I have that hollow feeling in my inside, you know; not the least hunger, but a horrid hollow feeling.

Charlotte.

(*entering* R *with the cutlet*) Godfather, here is your cutlet, nice and underdone.

Rabourdin.

Come along, child. Another piece of bread, Chapuzot.

Chapuzot.

(*taking up the bread, which he has rested on end against the sofa, and cutting off an enormous chunk. Aside*) There, if that does not choke him! (*Sits down again.*)

Charlotte.

(*passing the piece of bread to Rabourdin*) And now, godfather, shall I fry you a couple of eggs?

All.

Ah, no, no! what an idea!

Rabourdin.

Eh? And yet, fried eggs; not too well done, with a little pepper; that's light, that's easily digested.

All.

(*strenuously*) No!

Rabourdin.

(*resigning himself*) Well then, no, Charlotte. They love me, they feel that I could never get them down. (*Falls to at his cutlet.*) I should never be able to get them down. I am so weak, so weak! (*Charlotte goes out* C. *Madame Vaussard goes and sits down on the chair* L. *Madame Fiquet sits on the chair by the sofa.*)

Chapuzot.

(*aside*) That will finish him off.

Rabourdin.

It comes from seeing you there, my children. I forget my pain, in talking; I eat without thinking about it. Did not Eugénie come this morning? I thought I had seen her.

Madame Fiquet.

(*surprised*)   What! Eugénie?

Rabourdin.

Your daughter.

Madame Fiquet.

(*rising*)   Ah yes, my daughter.   She was here just now.   Where can she have got to?   (*Goes up stage*) Minette!   Minette!

Chapuzot.

(*grinning*)   Minette went back to the arbour long ago with Monsieur Ledoux.

Rabourdin.

Let her be, Lisbeth.   (*Madame Fiquet comes back and leans on his chair.*)   I am glad that the little pet comes and gets herself courted in my garden! Ah! family, family!   One is only happy in one's family!

Charlotte.

(*entering* R)   Godfather, there is a young man who is asking for you.

Rabourdin.

Do you know him?

Charlotte.

I have never seen him before.   He has a basket with him.

Rabourdin.

A basket?   Let him come in.   (*Charlotte beckons to Dominique, who enters R and walks straight up to Rabourdin, with outstretched hand.   Charlotte crosses up stage, and comes down L, laughing and waiting.*)

SCENE XI.

THE FORMER,   DOMINIQUE.

Dominique.

Good morning, uncle. (*Madame Vaussard springs up and runs towards her uncle, whom Madame Fiquet covers with her body. Chapuzot rises also, very anxiously.*)

Rabourdin.

(*surprised*) Eh ? (*Letting him take his hand*) Good-morning, my boy.

Madame Fiquet.

(*pushing Dominique aside*) You are at Monsieur Rabourdin's.

Dominique.

(*putting down his basket by the footlights*) I should think I was ! At my uncle Rabourdin's, one of the worthiest men in Senlis. (*Pushing Madame Fiquet aside in turn*) And are you in good health, uncle?

Rabourdin.

(*still surprised, and hesitating*) I'm very well indeed, my boy. I mean to say, I'm so-so—very so-so.

Madame Vaussard.

(*bending forward, lowering her voice*) It's some adventurer ! Do you know him ?

Rabourdin.

(*lowering his voice*) Not precisely. I am trying to recollect his face.

Dominique.

I am Dominique, the son of Long Lucas.

Rabourdin.

Dominique—Long Lucas. Yes!

Dominique.

You know, Long Lucas, of the farm, at Pressac.

Rabourdin.

The farm—at Pressac. Yes, yes.

Dominique.

And I am going to Paris to buy seeds. And so my father said to me, " Go and say good-day to your uncle Rabourdin, as you pass through Senlis. You shall take him a pair of ducks." Wait a moment, the ducks are in my basket. (*He takes out the ducks, and puts them on the table*) They're fine, fat ducks, uncle.

Rabourdin.

(*striking his forehead*) Why, of course, Long Lucas, of the farm at Pressac, he married—he married——

Dominique.

Mathurine Taillandier, the daughter of Jérôme Bonnardel.

Rabourdin.

That's it! (*He rises and shakes hands with Dominique. Charlotte stifles a laugh, and goes out* c) Ah, my nephew, how pleased I am to see you! And I said to myself, mind you, " You have seen that face before." You are the very image of one of my poor aunts. And are they all flourishing at the farm ?

Dominique.

Yes, thanks. And they send you their very kind regards. (*He takes his basket, and goes and sits down on the sofa, next to Chapuzot.*)

Rabourdin.

Consider yourself at home, make yourself comfortable. We are quite among ourselves here, all relations and friends. I am never happy till my house is full of people. (*He sits down again at the table, and resumes his sick man's voice*) I have much to comfort me in my last moments. Chapuzot, a piece of bread, please ; I am going to eat my strawberries.

Chapuzot.

(*rising*) With pleasure. (*He cuts a huge piece of bread. Aside*) Choke, old fellow, choke. (*Sits down again.*)

Madame Fiquet.

(*who has taken Madame Vaussard aside, up stage*) Mathurine Taillandier, Jérôme Bonnardel : do you know those names ?

Madame Vaussard.

(*low*) Never heard them. The young man's eyes glow like coals.

Madame Fiquet.

(*low*) We must watch him.

Charlotte.

(*entering* c) Godfather, here is Monsieur Isaac coming in through the garden.

Rabourdin.

(*very anxiously*) How unpleasant! We were so happy, all friends together.

Charlotte.

Here he is. (*She goes out* R, *Isaac enters* C, *Madame Fiquet moves away from the table.*)

SCENE XII.

MADAME VAUSSARD, RABOURDIN, MADAME
FIQUET, ISAAC, CHAPUZOT, DOMINIQUE.

Rabourdin.

(*while Madame Fiquet removes the napkin from his neck*)   Ah, there's that excellent Monsieur Isaac! I'm very bad, very bad, my poor Monsieur Isaac. You're as strong as a Turk, you are!

Isaac.

You're very kind.   I'm pretty well, thank you. I called about a little bill!

Rabourdin.

A little bill?

Isaac.

An outstanding account, two hundred and seventy-two francs, for a press.

Rabourdin.

What!   Haven't you been paid for that press yet? Really, if you did not know me——

Isaac.

Oh, I was in no way alarmed about it, Monsieur Rabourdin.   We know that you're good enough. I only wish you owed me a hundred times as much. (*Hands him the bill.*)

Rabourdin.

Two hundred and seventy-two francs.   (*He rises. Madame Vaussard has gone up stage and is sitting before the occasional table, turning over the leaves of an album.   Madame Fiquet is finishing her clearing away. Chapuzot is talking to Dominique.*) I don't know if I have any change. (*He feels in his pockets, and goes towards the safe.*) I felt sure I had taken the key of the safe from under my pillow. (*Getting angry*) It must be that scatterbrain of a Charlotte! I never know where to find anything in this house. (*Calling out*) Charlotte! Charlotte!

Madame Fiquet.

(*coming nearer to him, stretching out her hand to feel in his waistcoat pocket*) Perhaps the key is in your waistcoat pocket.

Rabourdin.

(*folding his dressing-gown closely about him*) Ah, no, I remember. It must have dropped out of my pocket yesterday, and I fear they will have swept it away, and thrown it into the street. (*Calling*) Charlotte! Charlotte! (*Fumbling on his person again*) Dear me, dear me, how annoying! (*To Isaac*) Are you in a hurry? Because otherwise I could send it you this afternoon.

Isaac.

I have plenty of time. (*The heirs, scenting a loan, turn their backs on Rabourdin. Madame Fiquet, who has carried the table behind the sofa, goes back to before the sideboard. Madame Vaussard puts the flowers into vases on the stove. Chapuzot continues to talk with Dominique, side by side on the sofa.*)

Rabourdin.

That's right. That's right! When one can't find a thing, you know, one loses one's head. (*Considering*) Not the slightest recollection. Everything seems muddled. Hang it all. Chapuzot!

Chapuzot.

(*turning round regretfully*) What is it, my friend?

Rabourdin.

You don't happen to have so much as that on you, I suppose?

Chapuzot.

No. (*Looking into his purse*) I have thirty-seven sous. I never carry any money. It's only in the way. (*Resumes his conversation with Dominique.*)

Rabourdin.

You're very wise. I just asked you on chance, to have done with it. Pray sit down, Monsieur Isaac. I may be some time.

Isaac.

Thank you. Don't mind about me.

Rabourdin.

We must try and find the money, damme! Thirty-seven sous, you said, Chapuzot? (*Chapuzot puts up his back without turning round.*) It's not thirty-seven francs? No : so much the worse. My dear Olympe, have you a few louis on you?

Madame Vaussard.

(*coming down stage looking vexed*) No, uncle, not so much as ten francs. I paid my dressmaker on my way here, and I have next to nothing left. (*Returns up stage.*)

Rabourdin.

Two hundred and seventy-two francs. We shall never get it together. And you, Lisbeth?

Madame Fiquet.

(*coming down stage with her basket*) Wait. I was

just looking to see. Sometimes I have a little money
hanging about. Money always drops down to the
bottom, among the crumbs. No, there are only
three four-sou pieces and a few centimes that the
baker gave me in change. (*Returns up stage.*)

Isaac.

(*coming forward*) I am bound to tell you that I
have a small payment to make this morning.

Rabourdin.

A small payment ! I know what that means,
a small payment! I simply must find that key.
Dear, oh dear, oh dear ! (*Goes up stage, holding his
head in his hands.*)

Dominique.

(*aside*) I feel sorry for the old boy ! (*Aloud, rising
from the sofa*) It is two hundred and seventy-two
francs, you say, uncle ?

Rabourdin.

(*surprised*) Yes, my boy.

Dominique.

(*handing him three bank-notes*) Here are three
hundred francs. (*All the heirs come down stage,
thunderstruck.*)

Rabourdin.

(*holding the notes in his hand*) Ah, my dear nephew !
my worthy nephew ! He has three hundred francs,
at his age ! I call that fine, that's very fine ! That
makes older people look small. Embrace me, my
boy ! You're a true Rabourdin ! Take it out of
that, Monsieur Isaac.

Chapuzot.

(*jabbering, in an undertone*)　What fools young men
are !

Madame Vaussard.

(*to Madame Fiquet, low*)　I don't like that lad !

Madame Fiquet.

(*low*)　Some scamp or other.

Isaac.

Hee, hee ! ready money makes ready friends.
There are your twenty-eight francs, Monsieur
Rabourdin.

Rabourdin.

Thanks, thanks.　(*He presses the hand which
Dominique holds out for the change, and puts the
money in his pocket.*)　We'll settle that, my boy.　I
remember things in my heart.　My family, that's
my life.　(*Growing affectionate*)　My poor children,
it shall all be repaid you at my death.　(*The heirs,
who have come up to him, lower their heads, and go
back.*)

Isaac.

It was not for that trifle I came.　I wanted to
show you some clocks.　You said you wanted one
for your bedroom.

Rabourdin.

A mere fancy.

Isaac.

(*handing him some photographs*)　I have some
photographs here.

Rabourdin.

Let's see.　(*Holding the photographs*)　Yes, indeed,.

those are handsome clocks. We might go and have a look at the chimney-piece. Come, all of you, and give me your opinion. (*He goes out on Dominique's arm. All follow him. As Isaac is about to go into the bedroom, he is held back by Madame Vaussard.*)

SCENE XIII.

MADAME VAUSSARD, ISAAC.

Madame Vaussard.
(*holding Isaac back*) I beg your pardon, Monsieur Isaac. Are you still as hard-hearted as yesterday? You can't refuse to renew those bills for me.

Isaac.
I am very sorry, really. But you have already renewed them five times. Why don't you get your uncle to pay me, as he is so fond of you?

Madame Vaussard.
(*quickly*) Not a word of this to my uncle! (*In a tone of conviction*) The reason I spoke to you again about these bills is that I thought that after having seen my poor uncle——

Isaac.
Hee, hee! he's full of life still.

Madame Vaussard.
Pooh! full of life!

Isaac.
Bless my soul, if I felt certain about it, I would not mind renewing once more. I would even let you have the three thousand francs you asked me for yesterday. You know I am not a hard man.

(*Crossing* L)   Only, as far as Daddy Rabourdin is
concerned—hee, hee!—I think you will have to kill
him with kindness, as the saying goes.   He is a
sturdy patient. (*Rabourdin cries off: "Monsieur Isaac!
Monsieur Isaac!"*) Excuse me, he is calling me. (*He
goes out* L.)

Madame Vaussard.

(*following him*)   What a wretch, that Isaac!   To
wait like that for an old man's last breath.

SCENE XIV.

MADAME FIQUET,   LEDOUX.

Madame Fiquet.

(*behind*)   Stay in the arbour, Minette!   (*Enters,
pushing Ledoux in before her.*)   There is no reason
why the poor darling should hear. (*To Ledoux*)
Yes, my cousin was letting you kiss her hand.

Ledoux.

I assure you, Madame——

Madame Fiquet.

You're a fool, see how you're blushing now!   I
am talking about this solely from the point of view
of our arrangements.   Yes or no, are you still
willing to marry my daughter Eugénie?

Ledoux.

I love Mademoiselle Eugénie, and if the hopes that
you have held out to me are realised——

Madame Fiquet.

Oh, not so many fine phrases.   I will give Eugénie
a hundred thousand francs to her dowry.   Besides,

if you are both of you very good, I will leave you the house. You would be comfortable here.

Ledoux.

I will take the liberty of observing to you, Madame, that we have not got so far yet. Monsieur Rabourdin——

Madame Fiquet.

He is as bad as he can be, my dear. And for the rest, my poor Minette can't wait any longer, or her uncle will understand. There are two matches already he has made her lose, and she is not far short of twenty-two.

Ledoux.

However, I think it would be as well to wait.

Madame Fiquet.

The marriage shall take place in September, at the latest. You must see if that suits you. We are worth, at least, a hundred thousand francs. Every marrying man in Senlis knows that. Oh, break it off, if you like. It's we who shall be the winners, Monsieur. (*Going up stage, and pointing to her basket*) I have memoranda there of a few husbands ; one has eighty thousand francs, another two hundred and twenty thousand, another two hundred thousand.

Ledoux.

No, stop, stop! I'll marry her. The thing is settled.

Madame Fiquet.

You'll marry her. The thing is settled. Shake hands on it. You can go back to Eugénie in the arbour. (*Ledoux goes out*, c.) Dear, oh dear, what a trouble those children are to me ! (*She sits down on the sofa.*)

SCENE XV.

RABOURDIN, CHAPUZOT, MADAME FIQUET, DOMINIQUE ; later ISAAC and MADAME VAUSSARD.

Rabourdin.

(*entering* L *with Chapuzot, still examining the photographs, while Dominique crosses and comes down stage* R) I think the Empire clock is a little too large. What do you say, Chapuzot ?

Chapuzot.

H'm, yes, I should prefer to have the Louis Seize clock on my mantelshelf. Take the Louis Seize clock, Rabourdin.

Madame Fiquet.

(*rising*) No, indeed ! I say the Louis Quinze clock ! A beautiful ornament for a bride's bedroom, if ever you want to make a present to one of your grandnieces. (*Goes up stage* R, *and puts on her bonnet and shawl.*)

Isaac.

(*entering with Madame Vaussard, who stays up stage* L, *putting on her hat*) The Louis Quinze style is the dearest. Twelve hundred francs.

Rabourdin.

Good heavens! (*Gives back the photographs to Isaac.*) Twelve hundred francs ! If I were to commit such an extravagance, I should think I was ruining my heirs.

Madame Fiquet and Madame Vaussard.
Oh, uncle!

Rabourdin.

(*reaching the door with Isaac*) And is your lowest price really twelve hundred francs? (*They go into the garden.*)

Chapuzot.

(*near the door, low*) He is madly anxious to have it.

Madame Fiquet.

(*low*) No, no, he would become too exacting! We must swear to one another not to run and buy it for him when we leave this.

Madame Vaussard.

(*low*) Let us swear: I am willing.

Chapuzot.

(*low*) Oh, there is no need for me to swear. Beware of the little nephew.

Rabourdin.

(*from the garden*) Are you coming, my children? (*They all three go out. Just as Dominique is about to follow them, he is stopped by Charlotte, who enters* R.)

SCENE XVI.

DOMINIQUE,   CHARLOTTE.

Charlotte.

Good-day, uncle! Good-day, nephew! Eh? What did I tell you? You were very comical, both of you.

Dominique.

Ah, I like your godfather. The poor old man appears to be so innocently preyed upon by those people. He was very embarrassed just now, when that Isaac came. He had lost the key of his safe.

Charlotte.

Oh, he had lost the key of his safe, had he?

Dominique.

You should have seen the faces of the others! They had not a sou amongst them. So then I played the swell, and brought out my three hundred francs.

Charlotte.

You lent my godfather three hundred francs?

Dominique.

Yes. He said he would settle it with me.

Charlotte.

(*bursting out*) Ah! no, no, godfather! I won't allow that! (*To Dominique*) And you, too, you're a fool!

Dominique.

But since he had lost the key of his safe!

Charlotte.

The key, the key! Hold your tongue! Look here, this is more than I can stand.

Dominique.

He will pay me back my money. I am quite sure of that.

Charlotte.

You have been robbed. There—now do you understand? It was my fault, I ought to have explained to you at once. But he will have to find you those three hundred francs, as sure as I'm born! And I want my dowry, my three thousand francs, this very evening!

Dominique.

Hush! Not before the people.

Rabourdin.

(*behind*) No, certainly not, Monsieur Isaac : you must not reckon on me.

Charlotte.

(*who has gone to fetch him, and who drags him in violently by his wrist across the stage towards his bedroom*) And now a word with you, godfather!

CURTAIN.

Act II.

Rabourdin's bedroom. At the back is a door leading into the dining-room; L of the door is a cupboard; R a bed hung with curtains. L U E is a window looking into the garden. L down stage is a door. R down stage is a chimneypiece decorated only with two candlesticks. There is the usual bedroom furniture, a night-table at the head of the bed, etc. Down stage L is an arm-chair, by the side of an occasional table; R another arm-chair.

SCENE I.

RABOURDIN,   CHARLOTTE.

(Charlotte opening the door C and dragging Rabourdin in violently by his wrist.)

Charlotte.
Are you not ashamed, godfather, to take that poor boy's three hundred francs!

Rabourdin.
Could I know? Put yourself in my place. He walks in, he says, " Good day, uncle." Naturally I concluded that he was my nephew.

Charlotte.

And you accepted the three hundred francs?

Rabourdin.

Well, since he was my nephew.

Charlotte.

You even kept the change.

Rabourdin.

Of course, since he was my nephew!

Charlotte.

But you knew all the time that you would never pay him that money back.

Rabourdin.

But, since he was my nephew! That will teach him to deceive people! You exposed your lover to all sorts of unpleasantnesses. Why, good gracious, I might have asked him for the clock.

Charlotte.

Don't let us lose our tempers. . . . You must at least give me my dowry.

Rabourdin.

(*nervously*)   Your dowry? Do you want your dowry?

Charlotte.

Of course, to get married with.

Rabourdin.

To get married with. Yes, yes, I see. My dear child, marriage is a very serious thing. You should reflect. You are too young, you know.

Charlotte.

I'm twenty.

Rabourdin.

How quickly little girls grow up! Twenty years old already! Besides, between ourselves, I don't like your intended. He looks a rake.

Charlotte.

Why, you thought him charming just now.

Rabourdin.

Pooh, charming. I am always prejudiced, you know, in my nephews' favour. But so soon as it concerns you, and your happiness——There is something in his look that I distrust. He would make you unhappy. (*Goes and sits down on the armchair* R.)

Charlotte.

I, unhappy with Dominique! Look here, godfather, don't make fun of me! I want my dowry.

Rabourdin.

Very well, I will give it you—the day you're married.

Charlotte.

I want my dowry at once.

Rabourdin.

(*pretending to laugh*) At once, do you hear that? Ah, no, mademoiselle, you can't have it at once.

Charlotte.

Godfather——

Rabourdin.

(*rising and crossing* L) You are absurd! You are so impulsive about all you do. Damme! you can't take back your money like that. I don't know what

I'm about—and suppose I had got rid of your
money?

Charlotte.

Godfather!

Rabourdin.

(*pretending to cry*)   They have taken everything
from me, my poor Charlotte; they have stripped me
bare, my scoundrelly heirs!

Charlotte.

(*shaking him*)   My dowry, my dowry!

Rabourdin.

It was they, I swear to you.

Charlotte.

That money was sacred, was it not?   You would
rather have dug the earth, you said, with your finger-
nails.

Rabourdin.

Yes, yes, dug the earth.   Oh, the rogues!   (*Sits
down in the arm-chair* L.)

Charlotte.

So that is over, we have not a sou left.   Dominique's
three hundred francs juggled away!   My aunt's
three thousand francs flown away!   And you think
I am going to accept that quietly?   No, indeed, I
would rouse all Senlis first.

Rabourdin.

You would be quite justified.

Charlotte.

I did not ruin you : I am not one of your nieces,
that you should revenge yourself on me by taking
my three thousand francs. (*Going to door* C *and*

calling out) Dominique! (*Dominique enters.*) And
we thought of taking the mill. All our dreams were
bound up in that money.

SCENE II.

RABOURDIN,   CHARLOTTE,   DOMINIQUE.

Rabourdin.

(*rising*)   There, there, my children, don't be so
distressed.   Money does not make happiness.   What
a couple of cherubims you will make!

Charlotte.

(*to Dominique*)   Do you hear that?   Pah! I had
guessed it.   Not a sou.   (*To Rabourdin*)   And now,
godfather, I want to know everything.

Dominique.

Speak to him gently.

Rabourdin.

Yes, she is bullying me.   When any one bullies
me, I always lose my head.

Charlotte.

No joking, please.   To whom did you give my
three thousand francs?

Rabourdin.

To whom?

Charlotte.

Yes, to which niece—to which nephew?   Out of
whose pocket am I to go and get it, that's what I
want to know?

Rabourdin.

Ah, if I could remember that.

Charlotte.

Old Chapuzot, may be ?

Rabourdin.

Yes, may be.

Charlotte.

That old nanny-goat of a Madame Fiquet ?

Rabourdin.

Possibly.

Charlotte.

Or that shrew of a Madame Vaussard ?

Rabourdin.

Well, well, I couldn't swear to it. (*Crosses, and goes up stage.*)

Charlotte.

But tell me plainly, yes or no ! (*To Dominique*) Do you see how he tries my patience ?

Dominique.

You are getting excited, you will do yourself harm.

Rabourdin.

(*coming down stage*) Well, I don't know : how can I know ? Five francs to one, five to the other, I suppose. The money went, without my guessing where it went to ! They had all combined to borrow from me, to suck me dry, to rob me. What I do know is, that they have drained me to my last farthing.

Charlotte.

There ! That pays us back, does it not ?

Rabourdin.

If I had your three thousand francs, I would give them back to you at once. I have never had any-

thing for myself. You will have this money sooner
or later. (*Growing touching*) All will be found there
after my death.

Charlotte.

Ah, no, that game won't do with me! I know
what will be found. So this money went amongst
the lot of them?

Rabourdin.

My poor children!

Charlotte.

Well, then, the lot of them will have to pay. As
sure as I'm born, they shall disgorge, or my name is
not Charlotte. (*Pushing Rabourdin violently into the
arm-chair* L) You—to begin with—just lie down
in that chair, and don't move from it.

Rabourdin.

Don't push me about. Why may I not move?

Charlotte.

(*To Dominique*) You next, you run to the friends,
the nephews, the nieces, and send them to me at
once. Tell them that Uncle Rabourdin is dying.

Rabourdin.

(*frightened*) Dying?

Charlotte.

Yes, dying! Tell them that he is spitting blood,
that he is delirious, that he can't hear nor see.

Rabourdin.

But no! No! I want to know——

Charlotte.

Oh, no explanations, do you hear? You will

just give up the ghost, that is what you have to do.
(*To Dominique*)   You understand?

Dominique.

Yes, I wish you luck.   (*Goes towards the door* c.)

Charlotte.

No, go that way.   (*Pointing to the door* L)   And
don't forget anybody, I want them all.

Dominique.

They shall be here within a quarter of an hour.
(*Goes out by door* R.)

SCENE III.

RABOURDIN,   CHARLOTTE.

Charlotte.

(*suiting the action to the word*)   And now to arrange
the room. It wants a little disorder. The bed-
clothes turned down, and dragging on the ground.
Clothes thrown about anyhow. Ah, a chair upset
near the door. That looks very well.

Rabourdin.

(*who has been watching these preparations, beseeching
her*)   If you would only tell me!

Charlotte.

Presently. I am first going to light the fire.
(*She lays and lights the fire.*)

Rabourdin.

Fire, in June! But I am too warm as it is, I
shall be suffocated. You will make me ill.

Charlotte.

That's all right.

Rabourdin.

What do you mean, that's all right?

Charlotte.

If you could have a nice fever, it would help us along splendidly. There now, let us see to the linseed tea. (*She takes a saucepan from the hearth, and puts it on the fire.*)

Rabourdin.

(*rising*) I won't drink any linseed tea.

Charlotte.

Leave off, you will drink it. (*Goes and looks on the night-table.*) What is this? Dandelion, the very thing! (*She empties the packet of dandelion into the saucepan*).

Rabourdin.

No, no—no dandelion! It's ridiculous, to take dandelion when one has eaten a good breakfast! It will swamp my inside. Besides, I am not going to drink it, in any case.

Charlotte.

You shall drink it, I tell you! (*Looking about her*) The room wants something more. There should be bottles, draughts, powders. Wait, I put the doctor's prescription in the drawer here. (*She takes the prescription from the drawer of the night-table.*)

Rabourdin.

You shall not go to the chemist.

Charlotte.

Certainly, I don't want to go. You have always a heap of filth in your cupboard. The first medicine that comes to hand will do. (*She goes to the cupboard* L, *climbs on a chair, and consults the prescription.*) Let us see. A mixture ! Here is one. Powders ! Here are a dozen untouched among your pocket-handkerchiefs. Pills ! Where on earth do you keep your pills ? Ah, I see a box under your vests. (*She springs off the chair.*) And a bath ! What a pity we haven't a bath. (*She places the medicines on the occasional table.*) In the meanwhile, you must take all this.

Rabourdin.

(*coming nearer*) I ! Never ! Do you mean to poison me ? Medicines that you pick up in a cupboard ! (*He crosses* L.)

Charlotte.

They are none the worse for that. You began them ; you can very well finish them, I should imagine.

Rabourdin.

No, I protest. You are abusing the situation.

Charlotte.

(*pushing him back into the arm-chair*) Will you sit down again ! And now, your shirt collar must look a little crumpled. That's it ! I am going to fetch you the quilt from your bed. (*She goes and fetches the quilt.*)

Rabourdin.

But I am suffocating, I tell you, I am suffocating ! I shall have an apoplectic stroke, I know.

Charlotte.

(*returning*) I can't help that, the quilt is essential.

(*She wraps him up.*)　There, now, lie out straight.
(*Kneeling before him*)　Don't you care to get back
your money, to make your heirs keep you ?

Rabourdin.

Yes, yes !　The rogues, I will take the last shirt
off their backs.

Charlotte.

Well, then, I will begin by making them give you
that clock that you so long to have.

Rabourdin.

Really, shall I have the clock ?

Charlotte.

You have only to die properly, I will look after
the rest.　The clock, the money—I want everything.
I mean to make your nieces remember me a long
time.

Rabourdin.

Ah, spare my heirs !　Don't skin them.　I leave
them in your hands.

Charlotte.

Don't be afraid !　Put back your head a little, half
open your lips, shut your eyes, pretend you can
neither see nor hear.　Very good, very good !
(*Stepping back and examining him*)　Oh, what a
fine dying man you make !　You look beautifully
ugly, godfather.　Take care !　(*Goes to the window.*)
It's Chapuzot.

Rabourdin.

The scamp !　Won't he be pleased !.

SCENE IV.

RABOURDIN, CHARLOTTE, CHAPUZOT.

Charlotte.

(*stopping Chapuzot, and throwing herself into his arms*) Oh dear, monsieur, it's all over ; hee, hee, hee ! (*She weeps.*)

Chapuzot.

Calm yourself, my child ! You see I am calm !

Charlotte.

(*stopping him again*) I was all alone, I was terribly frightened. I had to carry him here, and arrange him. And he has been there for half-an-hour—hee, hee, hee ! (*She weeps.*)

Chapuzot.

(*ridding himself of her, and going to look at Rabourdin*) Eh ! He is still breathing ! (*Leading Charlotte* R, *lowering his voice*) Well, and how did it happen ?

Charlotte.

It took him suddenly, after breakfast.

Chapuzot.

Yes, he ate like a wolf—huge chunks of bread.

Charlotte.

Then he turned quite pale.

Chapuzot.

Good !

Charlotte.

You could see the whites of his eyes.

Chapuzot.

Good !

Charlotte.

His cheeks turned cold, his tongue hung out.

Chapuzot.

Good, good!

Charlotte.

And he looked like a drowned cat, saving your presence.

Chapuzot.

Very good! But did he not bring up blood?

Charlotte.

Blood, good heaven! I thought he would not have a drop of blood left in. him. He is not able to move his little finger.

Chapuzot.

Capital! (*After a glance at Rabourdin*) And his voice? How was his voice? Very weak, was it not?

Charlotte.

Alas, my dear monsieur, he never spoke again!

Chapuzot.

(*delighted, very loudly*) Is that so? (*Lowering his voice*) My voice is so loud, do you think I disturb him?

Charlotte.

No, pray don't mind, he has lost his hearing and his eyesight.

Chapuzot.

(*approaching Rabourdin*) He can't hear, he can't see! Ah, the worthy man, the excellent man! (*Returning to Charlotte*) And my ears are so acute, my sight so sharp! Hee, hee! And nevertheless I am his elder!

Charlotte.

Don't compare yourself to my godfather. You could bury ten such as he. Eighty years old, what is that? It's when one is sixty that the serious illnesses show themselves, and that they carry you off. (*She crosses and places herself between Rabourdin and Chapuzot.*) Look at him in his arm-chair, and look at you, how straight you hold yourself, how firmly you stand, how your whole body glows with health and vigour!

Chapuzot.

You are right, my girl, I am in fine health. It is good to be well and strong! That old Rabourdin! How foolish of him to allow himself to drop so low! (*Lowering his voice*) This time, after such symptoms as those, I fear——

Charlotte.

Say rather that it is quite certain.

Chapuzot.

Eh? We need not fear to give ourselves up to our grief?

Charlotte.

No, we need not fear. Ah me!

Chapuzot.

(*coming up to Rabourdin and examining him*) His eyes are dead, he has not a drop of blood. (*Moving away, with his back turned, shivering*) He is cold already.

Rabourdin.

(*between his teeth*) You rascal of a Chapuzot!

Chapuzot.

(*turning round, alarmed*) Eh, didn't he speak?

Charlotte.
(*bringing him quickly before the footlights*)   Monsieur,
we never found that wretched key; I am embarrassed
for the small expenses.   Besides, I should not dare
to open the safe.   The money is yours now.

Chapuzot.
(*radiant*)   Mine !   That's true, the money is mine!
You dear girl !

Charlotte.
So I thought, instead of forcing the safe——

Chapuzot.
(*violently*)   I won't have my safe touched !   (*In a
hesitating voice, and going up stage, towards the
door* c)   I will give you something, if necessary.
Put the bills on one side, I will pay them; yes, I will
pay them—later on.   (*Coming down stage again, and
taking Charlotte aside*)   Do you think he will last
till to-night ?

Rabourdin.
(*between his teeth*)   You scoundrelly Chapuzot !

Chapuzot.
(*turning round, terrified*)   I will swear he moved.

Charlotte.
No, no, it was the quilt that slipped down.
(*Raising the quilt, low to Rabourdin*)   Keep quiet,
will you?

Rabourdin.
(*low*)   I'll fly at his throat, if you don't turn him
out!

Chapuzot.
What is he saying to you ?

Charlotte.

He is not saying anything, my dear monsieur. It's
the death-rattle in his throat, poor man. (*Returning*)
I was going to beg you, therefore, to lend me a few
hundred francs.

Chapuzot.

(*making for the door*) No, no, don't let us talk of
money, I feel too sad ; I am going to run for the
doctor, so that he may reassure us. Later on, later
on. (*He gets away, pursued by Charlotte.*)

SCENE V.

RABOURDIN,   CHARLOTTE.

Rabourdin.

(*bounding up and opening wide the door which Charlotte
has just closed*) Ah, you beast ! you beggar ! you
blackguard !

Charlotte.

(*closing the door*) Be quiet, he is still in the dining-
room.

Rabourdin.

Let me relieve my feelings. (*Re-opening the door*)
You good-for-nothing ! you scoundrel ! you cut-
throat !

Charlotte.

(*closing the door again*) Take care, you will spoil
all. There you are, as red as a peony.

Rabourdin.

(*coming down stage, gravely*) Have I any blood
under my skin : are you sure ?

Charlotte.

Certainly.

Rabourdin.

And are my eyes alive?

Charlotte.

Quite alive.

Rabourdin.

And is my tongue in its place?

Charlotte.

You seem well able to use it!

Rabourdin.

(*shaking his fist at the door*) You scum of the earth!
(*To Charlotte*) Just touch me, to see. How do I
feel? Am I cold?

Charlotte.

You are nice and warm, godfather.

Rabourdin.

(*relieved, letting himself go*) Ah, you do me good,
I breathe again. That highwayman of a Chapuzot
has such a self-convinced way of believing you dead
and buried! I was dying under that quilt, I had
pains all over me. He said, " My safe," that ghoul!
You will never get a sou out of that atrocious
carcase.

Charlotte.

(*who is looking out of the window*) Yes, yes, if you
will only have patience. (*She returns quickly, and
makes him sit down in the arm-chair, R.*)

Rabourdin.

I won't play the dead man any more, it makes
me too melancholy.

Charlotte.

Very well.   Sigh a little, godfather.   (*Rabourdin
sighs agreeably.*)   That's not it, that's a young lady's
sigh you're making!   Listen—harder, in this style.
(*She gives a mournful sigh*)   A rattle, a good rattle.

SCENE VI.

CHARLOTTE, MADAME FIQUET, LEDOUX, RABOURDIN, EUGENIE.

✓

⸢ Rabourdin.

(*with his eyes on the door*)   Oh dear, oh! how I
suffer !

Madame Fiquet.

(*coming down stage quickly, followed by the two young
people*)   So, it's true!   Poor uncle!   And we who
were just going out on business!   (*She keeps the
centre of the stage, after having put down her basket.
Ledoux and Eugénie lean over the back of Rabourdin's
chair, one* L, *the other* R.)

Rabourdin.

Ah !   Oh dear !

Eugénie.

Where does it pain you ?

Ledoux.

Is it in your chest?   Is it in your inside ?

Rabourdin.

Oh! oh !

Charlotte.

That is how he has been answering me the last
half-hour.   He utters nothing but that one cry.
You see the state the room is in.   It was a terrible

attack. I thought I should go mad. I am worn out. (*Sits down in the arm-chair* L.)

Rabourdin.

Oh! oh!

Madame Fiquet.

But we can't let him give over like this! We must bustle about. (*To Charlotte*) Have you nothing made hot—bricks, poultices, linseed-tea?

Charlotte.

There is some linseed-tea before the fire.

Madame Fiquet.

Quick then. Eugénie, give a cup of linseed-tea. (*Eugénie takes a cup from the fireplace, and fills it with linseed-tea.*)

Rabourdin.

Oh! oh! No, nothing, I am suffering too much.

Eugénie.

(*handing the cup to her mother*) Mother, it is boiling hot.

Madame Fiquet.

So much the better. Open your mouth, uncle.

Rabourdin.

(*tightening his lips*) No, I can't take it, I am choking.

Madame Fiquet.

He must drink it all the same. (*She makes him drink it in spite of himself.*) That is true, it was a little hot. (*To Rabourdin*) Well, does that warm you?

Rabourdin.

Oh! oh!

Madame Fiquet.

Another cupful, Eugénie.

Rabourdin.

(*dismayed*) I shall choke. No more linseed-tea, I implore you!

Madame Fiquet.

Sick people all talk like that. (*Going to the occasional table.*) And his mixture?

Charlotte.

It is more than an hour since he took it.

Madame Fiquet.

Good. (*Pours out the mixture into a spoon.*) There's a draught that does not smell nice.

Rabourdin.

Oh! oh!

Madame Fiquet.

(*to Ledoux*) Hold his head, Monsieur Ledoux. (*Turns to Rabourdin and shoves the spoon into his mouth.*) There!

Charlotte.

This is the time for his pills too. You can give him three.

Madame Fiquet.

(*going back to the occasional table*) Capital! (*To Ledoux*) Don't let go his head. (*Slips the pills into her hand.*) There are four of them. That will only do him so much the more good. (*Returns to Rabourdin, and makes him swallow the pills.*) He swallows them like an angel.

Rabourdin.

Pah! I'm choking! (*Coughs violently.*)

Madame Fiquet.

The linseed-tea, the linseed-tea! What are you about, Eugénie ?

Eugénie.

(*handing her a cup of linseed-tea*)   Here it is, mother.

Ledoux.

(*looking at the occasional table*)   There are some powders here——

Charlotte.

The powders are to put in the linseed-tea.

Madame Fiquet.

Capital! (*Ledoux empties a powder into the cup.*) What a funny colour. It won't be sweet enough. Look into my basket. Don't you see some sugar there ?

Ledoux.

(*going towards the night table*)   Two lumps, Madame Fiquet. (*He brings them to her.*)

Madame Fiquet.

(*with a friendly smile*)   It is the sugar from the coffee you gave us on Sunday. (*She puts the two lumps into the cup.*) Eugénie, help Monsieur Ledoux to hold him.

Rabourdin.

(*struggling*)   I'm better, I'm quite well—let me be !

Madame Fiquet.

(*after compelling him to drink*)   Ah, there's room for ten more like that.

Rabourdin.

Ah! Oh dear! Ah! Ah! I'm killed! (*He

*lets his head drop.   Then he falls asleep little by
little.*)

Eugénie.
I think he has fainted.

Ledoux.
He has taken enough.

Charlotte.
(*rising*) Yes, he seems to have had enough.   His
fainting-fit will relieve him.

Madame Fiquet.
Without doubt.   The linseed-tea has done him
an immense deal of good.   You see, he has left off
breathing.   That is what I wanted to bring about.
(*To Eugénie and Ledoux*)   Look after him, my
children, and if he complains again, don't hesitate—
linseed-tea !)(*The two lovers go up stage, slowly,
towards the bed, without giving any further attention
to Rabourdin.   Madame Fiquet takes Charlotte* L.)
When he saw himself approaching so near to his
end, did he say nothing important to you ?

Charlotte.
No.   Only, he never ceased talking of that clock.

Madame Fiquet.
The Louis Quinze clock ?   And what did he say
about it ?

Charlotte.
He spoke of it as though it were a friend, a real
person whom he would have longed to see by his
death-bed.   It would stand there, by his bed.   He
would watch the hands moving, he would feel less
alone in the world.

Madame Fiquet.
Yes.

Charlotte.
He doted thus like a lover, madame—I tell you these things because you are one of the family. It is one of those intimate details——

Madame Fiquet.
Go on, my child. There is no passion that I do not understand.

Charlotte.
(*very greatly overcome*) And then, he wanted it to strike his last hour.

Madame Fiquet.
His last hour——

Charlotte.
Alas, madame, his last hour!

Madame Fiquet.
And will he leave his fortune to the one who gives him the clock?

Charlotte.
Clearly he will leave his fortune to the person who——Ah! upon my word, you are sharper than I am.

Madame Fiquet.
It comes from being used to business. A word is enough for me. (*Calling*) Monsieur Ledoux!

Ledoux.
Madame.

Madame Fiquet.
(*taking him on one side, in the centre of the stage,*

while Charlotte goes up towards the cupboard, and Eugénie remains in front of the bed)   You have that money with you that you were going to invest, have you not?   Lend me twelve hundred francs.

Ledoux.

(*uneasily*)   But——

Madame Fiquet.

It is for something that I will explain later, which will make your marriage a certainty.

Ledoux.

(*hesitating, looking towards Rabourdin*)   Then, you think——

Madame Fiquet.

(*pointing to Rabourdin*)   But, my dear, just look at him.   The thing is obvious, the cash is ours—you must see that my daughter is able to choose for herself now.

Ledoux.

Here are the twelve hundred francs.   (*Hands her the money.*)

Madame Fiquet.

Good.   (*To Eugénie and Ledoux*)   My dears, look after your uncle, I shall be back presently.

Charlotte.

(*stopping her, up stage, in an undertone*)   Are you going to fetch the clock?

Madame Fiquet.

Not yet.   I want to make sure.   I will run round to the doctor's.   (*Exit.*)

SCENE VII.

CHARLOTTE, LEDOUX, EUGENIE, RABOURDIN.

Eugénie.

How warm it is here!

Ledoux.

It is stifling, Mademoiselle. Suppose we opened the window.

Eugénie.

(*crossing and going towards the window*) Yes, yes.

Charlotte.

No, I won't have a draught!

Ledoux.

(*approaching Eugénie, in an undertone*) We might go to the garden, Mademoiselle.

Eugénie.

(*looking out of the window*) No, I don't want to, I don't want to. At last, there is Mamma going down the street. Let us go into the garden, Monsieur Ledoux. (*They go out, smiling to one another.*)

SCENE VIII.

CHARLOTTE, RABOURDIN.

Charlotte.

They give no trouble, those lovers! One is never driven to show them the door. (*Going up to Rabourdin*) Eh, godfather? See! he does not move. Could he be dead in earnest? (*Stepping back*) I say, no joking—we were only in fun. Answer me, godfather—you know I am afraid of the dead.

(*Rabourdin gives a great snore. She comes nearer, laughing.*) My word! he has fallen asleep. He is snoring like a smith's bellows. Hi, godfather!

Rabourdin.
(*starting awake*) Eh, what? No linseed-tea! Look here, I am growing tired of this, I am as strong as a lion. (*Rises and passes* L.)

Charlotte.
(*laughing*) My poor godfather!

Rabourdin.
Ah, you are alone, mischief. And you made me swallow all that filth! Bah!

Charlotte.
(*running to the window*) Be quiet!

Rabourdin.
(*returning* R) That sleep has livened me up; I should have liked to take a little walk.

Charlotte:
Be quiet. (*She makes him sit down again*) Here they are with the doctor.

SCENE IX.

CHARLOTTE, MADAME FIQUET, MOURGUE, RABOURDIN, MADAME VAUSSARD.

Mourgue.
(*running up to Rabourdin, followed by the two women*) How now, my dear old friend? You were in pain, and I was not there!

Rabourdin.
Ah, doctor!

Mourgue.

Make yourself easy, I am here now, damme!
Your good health is my only concern. (*He takes
his pulse.*)

Madame Vaussard.

For goodness' sake, doctor, reassure us.

Mourgue.

(*gallantly*) I am at the orders of the Queen of
Senlis.

Madame Fiquet.

Give us some hope.

Mourgue.

In a minute. (*After a pause*) But he is as bad
as can be, I fear.

Rabourdin.

Worse than ever.

Mourgue.

Yes, very bad indeed. (*To the two women*) Calm
yourselves. (*Madame Fiquet, pondering, moves away
L, while Madame Vaussard stays near Rabourdin.*)

Charlotte.

(*coming nearer, to the doctor*) Shall I tell you,
monsieur, what symptoms showed themselves?

Mourgue.

It is not necessary, my dear. So long as you took
care that my prescription of this morning was well
carried out.

Charlotte.

Certainly, monsieur, he took them all. And it
was then that the crisis took place.

Mourgue.

Naturally. The remedies always shake the patient
up. Have you a pen and a sheet of paper? (*Charlotte takes from the occasional table a pen and a blotting-
book, and brings them to the doctor.*)

Rabourdin.

Another prescription, doctor?

Mourgue.

(*writing*) Oh, a mere nothing. Some syrup, a few
lozenges, some mineral water, some ointment, and
leeches. I lay stress upon the leeches—twenty-five,
do you hear?

Rabourdin.

(*uneasily*) No, no.

Charlotte.

Twenty-five leeches? One would say he has them
as it is.

Mourgue.

(*returning to Rabourdin*) There, my good friend,
you are looking better already. There is nothing
that cheers a sick man like a little prescription. By
the way, they told me that Chapuzot was running
after me. I caught sight of him, on my road here,
going bare-headed in the sun, looking wild, laughing
and singing like a drunken man. His condition
makes me feel very uneasy.

Rabourdin.

That good Chapuzot. It is his grief at seeing me
in such a bad way.

Madame Vaussard.

(*to Rabourdin*) You would do much better to go
to bed, uncle.

Charlotte.

(*low, to Madame Fiquet*)   Madame, I believe that nephew, that Dominique—the clock——

Madame Fiquet.

(*low*)   I had · forgotten it!   And he is not here, that's true!   I fly.   Not a word.   (*Goes out by the door* R, *so as not to be seen.*)

Charlotte.

(*aside*)   And now for the next one.

SCENE X.

CHARLOTTE, CHAPUZOT, MOURGUE, RABOUR-DIN, MADAME VAUSSARD.

Mourgue.

(*running towards Chapuzot, who staggers in, looking wild, and muttering*)   Ah!   what did I say?   (*To Charlotte*)   Help me, my dear.   (*They lead Chapuzot to the arm-chair* L.)

Chapuzot.

Nothing.   It is nothing—the sun—ah! that dear Rabourdin!   It affected me so!   Everything seemed to dance before my eyes.   (*Sits down.*)

Mourgue.

Let me take you back and put you to bed.

Chapuzot.

Me?   Get out!   I have never felt so lively.   Let me be, close his eyes, don't mind about me.   Oof! the excitement, the heat of the sun!   (*Faints away.*)

Mourgue.

I expected that.   Quick, some water, a wet towel. (*Goes up stage, looking for what he wants.*)

6

Rabourdin.

(*between his teeth*) If he could just perish before my eyes ! (*Groaning*) Ah! ah !

Madame Vaussard.

(*near Rabourdin* R) Good heavens, doctor, my uncle is dying !

Mourgue.

(*going to Rabourdin*) He should have a mustard poultice.

Charlotte.

(*near Chapuzot* L) Doctor, he does not breathe, I believe he is being suffocated.

Mourgue.

(*going to Chapuzot*) I will bleed him.

Madame Vaussard.

But, doctor, you can't let him die like this.

Mourgue.

(*going to Rabourdin*) I am at his service, fair lady.

Charlotte.

At least tell me what I am to do, doctor.

Mourgue.

(*going to Chapuzot*) This instant, my dear.

Madame Vaussard.

Doctor——

Charlotte.

Doctor——

Mourgue.

(*stopping in the centre, and wiping his forehead*) Spare me ! Science is powerless. I cannot save more than one at a time.

Rabourdin.

(*sighing*) Ah! ah! He so robust! To go before me! (*Mourgue busies himself about Rabourdin, Madame Vaussard goes up towards the bed.*)

Chapuzot.

(*recovering from his swoon*) Eh! he speaks!

Charlotte.

You have the shivers coming on. Would you like to be taken home? (*She goes up stage, watching Madame Vaussard.*)

Chapuzot.

No, I am very comfortable on this sofa. (*Glancing at Rabourdin, aside*) I will wait.

Charlotte.

(*up stage, low, to Madame Vaussard*) Madame, I think Madame Fiquet—the clock——

Madame Vaussard.

She has left the room, that's true! And here am I doing nothing! (*Goes out quickly* C.)

Charlotte.

(*aside*) That one of the two who returns empty-handed shall pay back my dowry.

SCENE XI.

CHAPUZOT, CHARLOTTE, MOURGUE, RABOURDIN, later MADAME FIQUET, later ISAAC.

Mourgue.

(*going from Chapuzot to Rabourdin*) As for me, I love the sick. Chapuzot, my friend, you are threatened, I tell you once again. Would you like to be covered up a little more, Rabourdin? You can't imagine how happy I am like this between my two dearest patients.

Rabourdin.

Poor Chapuzot!

Chapuzot.

Poor Rabourdin!

Madame Fiquet.

(*off stage*)   Wait there for a minute, I will call you in.   (*To Rabourdin*)   Uncle dear, will you be very good, very quiet?

Rabourdin.

I am as quiet as a lamb, my dear niece.

Madame Fiquet.

Will you be grateful to me, will you remember your Lisbeth later on?

Rabourdin.

Certainly.

Madame Fiquet.

Good news that I am afraid to tell you suddenly. (*To Mourgue*)   Can my uncle endure a great excitement, doctor?

Mourgue.

A great excitement—I should like to study the effect of a great excitement on him.   (*He takes his pulse.*)   Go on, Madame.

Charlotte.

(*going near Chapuzot*)   Wait, I will stand by the side of Monsieur Chapuzot, in case he should be overcome by the excitement.

Madame Fiquet.

(*up stage, on the threshold of the door* c)   Good, I

may proceed, may I not? (*Off stage*) Monsieur
Isaac, pray come in. (*Enter Isaac, carrying the
clock. He stops in the centre of the stage.*)

Rabourdin.

Ah, the clock, the lovely clock! (*Looks at it
delightedly.*)

Chapuzot.

(*between his teeth*)   It will give him a stroke.

Charlotte.

(*to Chapuzot*)   Take care of yourself, turn your
head away.

Rabourdin.

(*his eye still fixed on the clock*)   And it is mine, it
will live in my room!   Monsieur Isaac, I beg of
you, don't stir.

Isaac.

But it's breaking my arms.

Rabourdin.

How beautifully chased it is!

Madame Fiquet.

(*behind the chair, low*)   Well, doctor?

Mourgue.

(*very seriously, still holding Rabourdin's pulse*)   His
pulse is quick, he is gaining strength.

Rabourdin.

What perfection in the smallest detail!

Mourgue.

Capital! the muscles are coming into play again,
his life is returning to him.

Madame Fiquet.

(*aside*)   What!   Could he be recovering! (*Aloud*)

Put the clock on the chimney, Monsieur Isaac. (*Isaac crosses in front of Rabourdin, who follows the clock with his eyes.*)

Chapuzot.

(*between his teeth*) He looks as rosy as a young girl. Plague take him !

Rabourdin.

(*after Isaac has placed the clock on the mantel*) Near, oh! near—it is still more delightful !

Mourgue.

(*still holding Rabourdin's pulse*) The fever is all gone—only a little quivering, like the heart of a girl of fifteen beating for the first time.

Rabourdin.

(*turning to Madame Fiquet*) Thank you, Lisbeth.

Madame Fiquet.

Wait! (*With great intensity*) It strikes, uncle, it strikes!

Isaac.

(*who is regulating the clock*) Yes, the mechanism is in good order.

Madame Fiquet.

Alas ! my poor uncle! (*The clock strikes.*) A melancholy sound—oh dear !

Rabourdin.

It has a voice like a bird. (*The clock strikes again.*) It is like the music of spring-time. It strikes for life. Wait, let me wind it up myself. (*He forgets himself and runs to the mantel.*)

Madame Fiquet.

(*dumfoundered*) Now he is on his legs !

Chapuzot.

(*thunderstruck*)   On   his   legs!   (*He   has   a   fit,
Charlotte beats his hands.*)

Mourgue.

Very good.   That is the pills beginning to act.

Rabourdin.

(*very much embarrassed, pretending to stagger*)   Forgive   me—the   sudden   joy—I   thought   I   should   be
able.   Take   me   to   bed.   The   effort   has   been   too
great for me.   (*Madame Fiquet and Mourgue lead him
to the bed, and stay by his side.*)

SCENE XII.

THE SAME,   MADAME VAUSSARD.

Madame Vaussard.

(*on the threshold, aside*)   That's it, the clock is on
the chimney-piece.   What a trollop !   (*She stops Isaac
as he is going off.*)   I hope that, in the face of the
profound affliction with which I am threatened, you
will no longer make any difficulty about renewing
these bills.

Isaac.

None at all, madame.   We will add the customary
little interest.

Madame Vaussard.

And you will lend me the additional three thousand
francs?

Isaac.

Yes, I think I shall be able to lend them to you.
I will go and see your husband.

Madame Vaussard.

Do not trouble, he is at work, you would disturb him. Return here in an hour's time, I will have the necessary papers with me. (*Goes up stage and accompanies him to the door. Exit Isaac.*)

Charlotte.

(*who has heard everything, while pretending to be busy with Chapuzot*) Three thousand francs—the exact amount of my dowry!

Mourgue.

(*still before the bed*) Yes, my friend, turn round to the wall, endeavour to sleep. (*Comes down stage. Madame Vaussard comes nearer.*)

Madame Fiquet.

(*coming down stage, low to Mourgue*) A false hope, is it not? The last flicker of the lamp that is about to expire?

Mourgue.

No doubt. I will return in the evening, if necessary. (*Goes up stage, takes his hat and comes down again towards Chapuzot. Charlotte is in front of the bed. Madame Vaussard and Madame Fiquet are standing* R *down stage, exchanging ferocious glances.*) Chapuzot, you ought to go to bed.

Chapuzot.

Eh, what? No, damme! you shan't get me away. I consent to take a little air in the garden, but that is all.

Mourgue.

Well, come to the garden. (*Offers him his arm.*)

Chapuzot.

(*struggling*) Let me be ; I could carry you on my back, if I liked. (*He has a fit, and falls into the arms of Mourgue, who drags him off.*)

SCENE XIII.

MADAME VAUSSARD, MADAME FIQUET, CHAR-
LOTTE, in front of the bed, RABOURDIN, lying on the bed.

Madame Vaussard.

(*furiously and very loud*) We ought not to make him such presents as that. It was you who proposed to swear——

Charlotte.

(*placing herself between them*) Gently, gently, ladies, my godfather is dozing. (*Returns to the bed and draws the curtains.*)

Madame Vaussard.

(*continuing in a lower voice*) It was just a trap, neither more nor less.

Madame Fiquet.

(*low*) I was quicker than the others, that is all.

Madame Vaussard.

Say, rather, you had less delicacy.

Madame Fiquet.

Bah, you were close upon my heels ! Each one for himself. So much the worse for you if your fal-lals prevented you from running.

Madame Vaussard.

(*raising her voice little by little*) My fal-lals ! Now

you are going to insult me! I won't follow you on that ground. I will find another present for my uncle.

Madame Fiquet.

(*raising her voice little by little*) That's right.

Madame Vaussard.

A handsomer present than yours—less absurd, and in better taste.

Madame Fiquet.

As you please. I will buy him a dearer one.

Madame Vaussard.

And I, one dearer than that.

Madame Fiquet.

And I one dearer still.

Madame Vaussard.

(*very loud*) Madame!

Madame Fiquet.

(*very loud*) Madame!

Charlotte.

(*placing herself between them again*) For goodness' sake, go into the garden. He is asleep.

Madame Fiquet.

(*taking Charlotte aside*) It's that hypocrite! I shan't go if she stays. (*Low*) Influence your god-father in my favour, and your fortune is made. (*Goes up stage.*)

Madame Vaussard.

(*taking Charlotte aside*) The shameless woman! I refuse to go till she does. (*Low*) I reckon on you, child; I will reward you.

Madame Fiquet.

(*before the door*) Pray go first, Madame.

Madame Vaussard.

(*same business*) Madame, after you.

Charlotte.

(*pushing them both out*) Oh, get out, the two of you!

SCENE XIV.

CHARLOTTE, RABOURDIN, later DOMINIQUE.

Charlotte.

One can't breathe with two gossips like those on one's hands.

Rabourdin.

(*putting his head cautiously between the curtains*) Nobody! Eh, Charlotte!

Charlotte.

What, godfather?

Rabourdin.

No nieces left; are you sure? Eh, behind the chairs, under the furniture?

Charlotte.

No, they are all in the garden.

Rabourdin.

Then—(*He jumps off the bed.*) Wait, the bolt, to make sure. (*Pushes the bolt, and comes back pirouetting*) Houp-la, houp-la! that does me good. Houp-la! my legs are quite stiff, on my word.

Charlotte.

Take care, they will hear you!

Rabourdin.

What do I care? I've got the clock. (*He takes*

her by the waist and forces her to waltz with him,
humming)   I've got the clock !   I've got the clock !

Charlotte.

Do stop—I haven't got my dowry yet !   Chapu-
zot and Madame Vaussard will have to disburse.
(*She hears a knock at door* R.)   There is Dominique.
(*She goes and opens the door, and admits Dominique.*)

Rabourdin.

(*who has gone to admire the clock*)   Charming !   It
is true I deserve it after all I have gone through
this morning.

Dominique.

(*quietly*)   It is not yours yet.

Rabourdin.

(*turning round, very uneasily*)   What's that ?   What
does my nephew say ?

Dominique.

I say that I know the bargain that was concluded
between your niece Fiquet and Master Isaac.

Rabourdin.

Well !   She bought the clock for twelve hundred
francs.

Dominique.

No, she hired it, till this evening, for ten francs.
You understand, uncle—this evening you will be
dead.

Rabourdin.

(*dumfoundered*)   This evening I shall be dead.   (*Under-
standing*)   Ah, the trickster !   I recognise her by that
touch !

Charlotte.
(*laughing*)   My poor godfather !

Rabourdin.
(*exasperated*)   I am robbed, I am murdered.   (*Crossing and sitting down* R)   Listen, Charlotte : torture them, ruin them, give them some illness that shall carry them off with fury.   I will make you a present of the clock if you get it out of them.

Charlotte.
It's a bargain.   But we must first satisfy your excellent relations.

Rabourdin.
Satisfy them !   No bad jokes, do you hear ?   (*The clock strikes.*)

Charlotte.
(*stretching her hand towards the clock*)   It is striking your last hour, godfather.   (*Rabourdin springs up with an air of alarm.   Then all are seized with a fit of mad laughter.*)

CURTAIN.

Act III.

The Scene is the same as in Act 1. When the curtain rises, Madame Fiquet and Madame Vaussard are discovered seated at the two sides of the round table, the first L, *the other* R. *Madame Fiquet is sorting papers, which she draws from her basket ; Madame Vaussard is engaged in writing ; Chapuzot leans against the safe* L, *and talks with Dominique ; Ledoux and Eugénie, seated side by side on the sofa* R, *whisper to one another, smiling.*

SCENE I.

CHAPUZOT, DOMINIQUE, MADAME FIQUET, MADAME VAUSSARD, LEDOUX, and EUGENIE.
This whole Scene is spoken in an undertone.

Madame Fiquet.
(*stopping in her work, in order to listen*) I thought I heard a deep sigh.

All.
(*looking towards the door of the bedroom, which is standing wide open*) A deep sigh?

Madame Fiquet.
Yes, like a breeze passing over my back. Wait !

(*She rises and goes to the door* L ; *she calls softly*)
Charlotte!

Charlotte.

(*appearing on the threshold*)   Hush!

Madame Fiquet.

Nothing new ?

Charlotte.

(*in a very low voice*) Ah, Lord! It is nearly
over.   Do not come in, the least noise irritates him.

Madame Fiquet.

Is the doctor still there ?

Charlotte.

Yes, yes.   Hush! (*All the heirs shrug their
shoulders, and turn their backs to the door.*)

Madame Vaussard.

(*bitterly to Madame Fiquet, who returns to her seat*)
That is the fourth time that you have excited us for
nothing.   (*They both resume their occupations.*)

Chapuzot.

It is enough to give me a stroke—it's absurd.

Dominique.

Let us sit down.

Chapuzot.

No, the air has brought me to, I am very comfortable, leaning like this. (*He caresses the safe
with his hand as he speaks.*)   I was telling you that
the house——(*Dominique signs to him to speak lower.*)
Yes, yes ; the house——(*He continues in a whisper*)

Ledoux.

(*tenderly*)   This day, mademoiselle, is the happiest of
my life.

Eugénie.

(*simpering*) Ah, Monsieur Ledoux, really.

Ledoux.

I have passed the whole of it in your company,
and you have graciously confessed that you love me.

Eugénie.

Mamma allowed me to make that avowal.

Madame Fiquet.

(*without raising her head*) Listen, she is giving
him something to drink. I can hear the sound of
the spoon in the cup.

Chapuzot.

(*without looking towards the door*) It is something
with sugar in it. She has taken the sugar-bowl from
the night-table.

Madame Vaussard.

(*without ceasing to write*) No, from the cupboard.
The cupboard-door creaked.

Eugénie.

(*continuing, to Ledoux*) Mamma gave me leave to
grant you my hand, since my poor uncle——

Ledoux.

You are an angel. (*He kisses her hand.*)

Eugénie.

Mamma assures me that between the two of us we
shall have nearly twenty thousand francs a year. I
have such plans—oh! such plans. I want a drawing-
room much finer than my aunt Vaussard's; I want a
lady's maid; I want six new dresses every year, a
little carriage, a little horse, a little country-house.

Ledoux.

Of course, everything that will give you pleasure, my adorable Eugénie. Jewels, laces——

Eugénie.

(*very joyously*) Yes, yes ; jewels, laces. (*Changing her voice*) Mamma said you might kiss me on the forehead.

Madame Vaussard.

(*raising her head quickly*) This time.

All.

(*turning towards the door*) What?

Madame Fiquet.

(*listening*) No, no, it is Charlotte blowing the fire.

Charlotte.

(*springing in, crossing up stage*) Warm towels! warm towels! I have let the fire out. The poor man is frozen! (*She goes into the kitchen* R.)

Madame Vaussard.

(*after hesitating*) I have only a few lines more to write. (*She resumes her work.*)

Madame Fiquet.

(*same business*) I should like just to finish putting this basket in order.

Ledoux.

(*to Eugénie*) Your forehead is as pure as a spring morning. (*He kisses her again.*)

Eugénie.

Gently—kiss me gently, so that we may not disturb anybody. (*They continue to whisper together.*)

7

Chapuzot.

(*raising his voice slightly, and coming down stage with Dominique*) No, iron borders are very ugly. I prefer box. I will put box everywhere, I will have those walks that want it sanded, and I will trim the lilac bushes here and there. In that way I shall have a pretty garden.

Dominique.

A very charming garden.

Chapuzot.

Rabourdin never had any taste. (*They go up stage.*) Look, you can see from here, on the right, at the end of the pathway, that big elm, in whose shadow nothing can grow. Well, I shall have it cut down. To-morrow it will be gone. I want to be able to enjoy my garden in the sunshine. (*They come down stage*). Then, behind the house, I mean to plant a large orchard. In ten years' time I shall be eating the finest fruit in Senlis.

Charlotte.

(*crossing the stage, and going into the bedroom L with a towel folded over her hands*) It burns me. Warm some towels. I have lit three fires.

Madame Vaussard.

(*in a vexed voice*) I wish, my dear, you would stop going to and fro. You make such a draught with your petticoats!

Madame Fiquet.

Or at least shut the door. (*She rises and shuts the kitchen door* R.) We are right in a draught, we shall all catch cold. (*Goes and sits down again.*)

Eugénie.

(*smiling, her hand in both Ledoux'*) My dream is a room in blue satin, with lace embroidery. Flowers everywhere.

Ledoux.

You shall have everything you like, my adorable Eugénie.

Madame Fiquet.

(*continuing the inventory of her basket, between her teeth*) I shall never get done. I was saying, the register of that little woman, the protested bill of that young man, the petition of the gentleman who discovered his wife——

Chapuzot.

(*to Dominique, with whom he goes up stage*) You see, the walls are sound, the woodwork is in good condition. (*They go out into the garden, after Isaac has entered.*)

SCENE II.

MADAME FIQUET, ISAAC, MADAME VAUSSARD, LEDOUX, EUGENIE; CHAPUZOT and DOMINIQUE, *whom one sees for a moment at a time in the garden.*

Isaac.

(*coming up to Madame Vaussard, who is still writing*) Madame!

Madame Vaussard.

One moment, Monsieur Isaac. I am just finishing our little business. (*She continues to write.*)

Madame Fiquet.

(*tumbling all her papers back into her bag*) Bother!

I must try to get them straight some other day.
(*Taking Isaac aside* L)   You can come and fetch the
clock away this evening.

Isaac.
Very well, madame.

Madame Fiquet.
Or if you care to wait——You know I am marrying
my daughter.   The dear child!   (*She looks at Eugénie
just as Ledoux is kissing her.*)   Your hands and forehead only, Eugénie.

Charlotte.
(*off stage*)   Somebody!

All.
(*looking towards the bedroom door*)   Eh ?

Charlotte.
(*coming on*)   Somebody, quick!   Run to the chemist
for a mixture!

Madame Fiquet.
How you startled us!   (*The heirs put on an air of
annoyance.   Chapuzot and Dominique return to the
garden.   Ledoux, who has risen, stands leaning against
the back of the sofa.   Madame Fiquet continues,
lowering her voice.*)   Eh! you need not disturb anybody.   In the position where our uncle now is—
(*taking the medicine bottle, and filling it with water
from a water-bottle standing on the sideboard*)—what
is the use of spending money, eh ?   This is just
as good.

Charlotte.
Give it here.   (*She takes the water-bottle, and
returns to the bedroom.*)

Madame Fiquet.

If one listened to sick people, they would swallow down a whole chemist's shop. (*She goes up stage, and talks to Chapuzot and Dominique.*)

Madame Vaussard.

(*rising, leading Isaac down to the footlights*) Here. My husband was busy. I made him sign the blank bills, and I filled them up myself.

Isaac.

You see, I have not yet quite decided.

Madame Vaussard.

What do you mean? You gave me your word!

Isaac.

No doubt, I did promise. (*Looking towards the door of the bedroom*) But there are so many risks to be run. (*Crosses* R.)

Madame Vaussard.

Well, keep your money, I shall have no difficulty now. I will find another money-lender. The interest is good enough.

Mourgue.

(*on the threshold of the bedroom door*) There is nothing more to be done, my child, nothing but to await the end.

Isaac.

(*holding Madame Vaussard back*) Madame, here are the three thousand francs. (*Hands them to her in bank-notes, and goes out* c. *Chapuzot, Dominique and Madame Fiquet come down stage with Mourgue.*

SCENE III.

CHAPUZOT,   MADAME   FIQUET,   MOURGUE,
MADAME VAUSSARD, LEDOUX, EUGENIE,
and DOMINIQUE *up stage* L, *hiding, so as to
be able to laugh.*

All.

Well?

Mourgue.

A most curious case, an inexplicable illness.

Chapuzot.

Really.

Mourgue.

An insidious complaint affecting every part at the
same time, and yet I cannot catch the nature of it.

Madame Vaussard.

Good gracious!

Mourgue.

An extraordinary disease which baffles me, old
practitioner as I am. It is very serious, very serious,
very serious!

Chapuzot.

(*coming up to the doctor*) Old age, doctor. I have
heard that at Rabourdin's age one's limbs swell, and
one dies of suffocation.

Mourgue.

Very serious, very serious, very serious. (*Chapuzot
goes up stage.*)

Madame Fiquet.

Then, doctor——

Mourgue.

I am nonplussed. Science has such depths. (*He looks at his watch.*) Egad! it's six o'clock, I must go to dinner. Mesdames, and everybody, good evening. (*He goes out bowing, and kissing the hand of Madame Vaussard.*)

SCENE IV.

CHAPUZOT, DOMINIQUE, MADAME FIQUET, MADAME VAUSSARD, EUGENIE, LEDOUX.

Dominique.

Are you not going to dinner, Monsieur Chapuzot?

Chapuzot.

No, I shall be brave to the end. (*Returns and leans with his back against the safe.*) I confess, nevertheless, that my inside——

Madame Fiquet.

(*resuming her seat at the table* L, *whilst Madame Vaussard returns to hers* R) No doubt it is dinner-time. Are you hungry, Minette?

Eugénie.

A little, mamma. I would like something. If there were only some cakes !

Charlotte.

(*off stage*) Oh dear ! oh dear !

All.

(*rising*) What ?

Charlotte.

(*off stage*) He is dead !

All.
(*without moving, as though transfixed*)   Dead!   (*A long pause.*)

Madame Vaussard.
(*uttering three sobs, which she stifles in her pocket-handkerchief*)   Ha! ha! ha!

Madame Fiquet.
I can't cry.

Chapuzot.
No more can I.

Madame Fiquet.
My tears are all inside.

Chapuzot.
So are mine.   It shows that one suffers much more.

Madame Fiquet.
(*turning to Eugénie*).   Cry, Minette, cry, it will relieve you.

Eugénie.
(*crying*)   Hee! hee! hee!

Madame Fiquet.
How I envy you being able to cry!   (*To Ledoux*) Take her into the garden, Monsieur Ledoux, try to distract her thoughts.   (*Madame Vaussard has crossed* R, *Madame Fiquet recalls Eugénie*)   Eugénie, you poor child, you have no longer an uncle. (*Lower*)   You may let him kiss your cheek. (*Ledoux and Eugénie go out.*)

Dominique.
(*removing the chair that stands at the head of the*

table) There are certain formalities to be gone through.

Madame Vaussard.
Such a kind-hearted man !

Madame Fiquet.
(*coming down stage*)   Such a good business head

Chapuzot.
A friend of forty years' standing !

Dominique.
We ought to go to the Mayor's.

Chapuzot.
And do you remember how lively he was, before his illness made him unbearable?

Madame Fiquet.
He had such touching fancies. I seem still to hear him talking of his approaching end !

Madame Vaussard.
And he expired as he said he would—that great, generous, noble heart !

Dominique.
(*removing the table, which he places behind the sofa*) We ought also to think of sending out the notices.

Madame Fiquet.
(*pulling a face*)   Ah, tears, here come my tears ! *The three heirs weep, spreading out their pocket-hand-kerchiefs.*)

Dominique.
(*coming down stage*)   Ah, calm yourselves. He is dead now, it is all over. Let us be business-like.

Madame Fiquet.

(*wiping her eyes ; in a deliberate voice*) You are right, let us be business-like. (*They all three replace their pocket-handkerchiefs in their pockets.*)

Chapuzot.

We are not a pack of children.

Madame Vaussard.

Our tears will not bring him back to us.

Chapuzot.

No, indeed. I will look after the letters to be sent out. (*Goes up stage, and stops near the sideboard.*)

Madame Fiquet.

(*to Dominique*) You, young man, had better go and notify the death at the Mayor's.

Dominique.

Very well, madame. (*He goes out c.*)

Madame Vaussard.

My mourning is quite ready, I will run and put it on. (*Goes out c.*)

Madame Fiquet.

I will go and see to the kitchen. We shall want some mulled wine for the watching. (*Goes out through the kitchen.*)

SCENE V.

CHAPUZOT, later CHARLOTTE.

Chapuzot.

(*by the sideboard*) Did they want to get rid of me ? They are capable of putting my house in their pockets, those gossips! (*Taking a tray from the sideboard*) See, here is the silver tray I gave Rabourdin. I don't see why I should leave it about. (*He slips the tray into his pocket.*) I must keep an eye on Fiquet's basket; she might take away things in it. (*Looking about him.*) And the gold-knobbed stick, where is it? I can't see it. Ah, here it is. (*He goes and fetches it from near the safe, and returns with short steps.*) It cost me sixty francs. (*Charlotte enters laughing, while he endeavours to hide it under his coat.*) Damn! the end sticks out! I'll take the knob off, at least. (*While he is trying to force off the knob, Charlotte touches him on the shoulder. He starts, frightened, and turns round, quaking.*) Eh, Rabourdin!—Ah, it is you, my dear! What do you want? (*Makes vain efforts to hide the cane.*)

Charlotte.

Now that everything is yours, monsieur, I thought you might like to give me that money of which I spoke to you, rather than force open the safe.

Chapuzot.

Very well, very well. Would fifty francs be enough?

Charlotte.

Oh, no, there are all kinds of expenses. Give me three hundred francs.

Chapuzot.

Goodness gracious! Three hundred francs! I should have to go home to fetch it.

Charlotte.

Well?

Chapuzot.

Why, if I were to go away from here they might steal all my things.

Charlotte.

Am I not here? I will keep good watch, I promise you.

Chapuzot.

You won't stir from the safe? (*He pushes her against the safe*) You will stay there?

Charlotte.

I swear.

Chapuzot.

(*stroking the safe*) Ah, how soft and warm it is! I will run and come back at once. (*He hurries off and stumbles as he goes.*)

Charlotte.

Take care, come back whole. (*Charlotte drops into the chair* L, *seized with a wild fit of laughter*) Ha! ha! ha!

SCENE VI.

CHARLOTTE,   MADAME FIQUET.

Madame Fiquet.

What's that? I heard laughter.

Charlotte.

(*crying*) Hee, hee, hee.

Madame Fiquet.

Was it you crying? Tears sound strange at a distance. The kitchen is topsy-turvy. We shall want some soup, some coffee, something hot. (*She*

fumbles about in the sideboard and brings out a bottle.)
What is this?

Charlotte.
Rum, madame.

Madame Fiquet.
H'm, I'll take a drop! I feel a wreck. (*She
pours out and drinks a drop, and then goes towards
the bedroom.*) And now it is time to attend to——

Charlotte.
(*rising and crossing* R) Go in, madame. You owe
him those last offices. He has left you everything.

Madame Fiquet.
(*on the threshold*) Really? (*She returns towards
Charlotte.*)

Charlotte.
As true as that the poor dear man is no more.
He made his will just now, while you were in the
garden. I dipped the pen into the ink for him
myself.

Madame Fiquet.
And do I get everything—the furniture, the
house, the money?

Charlotte.
Everything, madame. I said a good word for
you. You promised you would not forget me if I
did.

Madame Fiquet.
Ah, so now the requests for money are commencing,
eh? As soon as people know that I have money
they want to put their hands into my pockets. (*She
crosses* R.) Well, I won't have it. I suppose you

thought that I was going to keep you for the rest
of your life ?   Listen : if you are of any further use
to me, I will give you six fine linen chemises.   That's
a bargain.

Charlotte.
Thank you, madame.

Madame Fiquet.
(*crossing, and going once more towards the bedroom*)
And now you can help me carry away the clock.

Charlotte.
(*following her*)   The clock !   But why carry it
away ?   Surely you bought it ?

Madame Fiquet.
(*conceitedly*)   Of course !

Charlotte.
(*turning as though to go into the bedroom*)   Oh, I
have no objection.   It is your own look-out.   Let
us fetch the clock.

Madame Fiquet.
You say that in an odd voice.

Charlotte.
(*returning* R)   No ! no !   You pay too badly for
what one does for you.

Madame Fiquet.
Look here, I like being generous in business—I
will make it a dozen.   What is it ?   Tell me all.

Charlotte.
No ! a thousand times no !   It makes no difference
to me if you pitch your inheritance out of the
window !

Madame Fiquet.
Eh ?

Charlotte.
What do I care if the will is made invalid ?

Madame Fiquet.
How invalid ?

Charlotte.
The clause says distinctly the inheritance belongs to the person who bought the clock.

Madame Fiquet.
But that clause is idiotic! My uncle has always had a weak head ; all Senlis can bear witness to that, if wanted. I shall go to law! Yes, I shall go to law! That Rabourdin was a spiteful creature.

Charlotte.
Well, he had his strange periods.

Madame Fiquet.
Wicked, obstinate, hypocritical! What shall I do ?

Charlotte.
Well, it's all over. You won't get a sou !

Madame Fiquet.
(*furiously*) Hold your tongue, you fool! When one is used to business——(*Reflecting*) Of course, that's the thing. Wait for me here. You've got the sense to wait for me, at least? (*Going out* c) Dear me, what a fool that girl is !

SCENE VII.

CHARLOTTE,   MADAME VAUSSARD.

Madame Vaussard.

(*in a very handsome black dress, following Madame Fiquet with her eyes*)   Where is my cousin running so fast?

Charlotte.

(*looking at her dress, pretending to be very deeply moved*)   Forgive me—the emotion of seeing you in mourning——(*Changing her voice*)   Dear me! how well black suits you!

Madame Vaussard.

(*displaying herself*)   Do you think so?

Charlotte.

And what an exquisite dress!   These little flounces are so sweet!   (*She turns round her.*)

Madame Vaussard.

(*crossing* R)   I thought I would have silk; stuff would have looked rather sad.   And the lace?   You don't think there is too much lace?   (*She returns* L.)

Charlotte.

No, not at all.   One does not go into mourning to make oneself look a fright.

Madame Vaussard.

(*mournfully*)   Ah, the real mourning is that which we wear in our hearts.   (*Changing her voice*)   I have been closeted with my dressmaker for more than a fortnight.

Charlotte.

(*clapping her hands*)   It's lovely! lovely!   What a

sensation that dress will make at the funeral. (*Sniffling*) At the funeral, madame, the funeral; ah me!

Madame Vaussard.

(*drawing out a splendid embroidered handkerchief to dry her eyes*) At the funeral, my poor dear! (*Changing her voice*) But where was my cousin running off to? She seemed very excited.

Charlotte.

I should think she had reason to be uneasy.

Madame Vaussard.

So our kind uncle——?

Charlotte.

(*confidentially*) I promised to do my best for you. He declared in his will that he would leave all his fortune to that one of his heirs who would have the generous thought to bury him with all possible magnificence. Have you that generous thought, madame?

Madame Vaussard.

Of course, since years. (*In an undertone*) That will cost me a deal of money.

Charlotte.

Ah, but, you know, he expects the very finest funeral to be had for money—everything perfect: mass at the high altar, three hundred francs for candles.

Madame Vaussard.

(*crossing* R) Three hundred francs, great heavens One hundred will be enough.

Charlotte.

Five hundred francs to the poor.

Madame Vaussard.

That is madness! He will ruin me.

Charlotte.

Then the embalming.

Madame Vaussard.

(*crossing* L) Have him embalmed! Never!

Charlotte.

The embalming. Three thousand francs in all. The will says three thousand francs.

Madame Vaussard.

(*thunderstruck*) Three thousand francs! I would rather not inherit.

Charlotte.

In that case, madame, I think you will be satisfied. That young man, that nephew from nobody knows where——

Madame Vaussard.

He told me he was going to the registrar's, the little wretch! (*In despair*) But then I am robbed. He might possibly, on his road——(*Taking a paper from her pocket*) Help me in this, I beg you.

Charlotte.

It has only to be ordered.

Madame Vaussard.

No, I want to pay for it now. The nephew might be before me otherwise. It is shocking, to have to spend so much money on a dead man!

Charlotte.

(*eyeing the bank-notes which Madame Vaussard holds in her hand*)　And Senlis, madame—Senlis will be talking of your generosity ten years hence.　Senlis will never have seen such a funeral.　You will be greeted, respected, renowned.

Madame Vaussard.

(*self-satisfied, crossing* R)　Yes, I shall deserve some esteem.　I shall be overwhelmed with visits.　I am sure the wife of the notary and the town-clerk's two daughters will die of envy.　(*Charlotte snatches the bank-notes from her.*)　Take care you don't lose those three thousand francs.

Charlotte.

(*slipping the notes into her dress*)　Have no fear, they will stay there.　(*She makes as though she would go out, when Madame Fiquet comes in, and takes her aside.*)

SCENE VIII.

MADAME FIQUET, CHARLOTTE, MADAME VAUSSARD.

Madame Fiquet.

(*taking Charlotte* R, *in an undertone*)　I've bought the clock.　It was so simple!　But this is more ingenious.　(*She puts a piece of paper into her hand*)　Take it.　You must slip this in among your uncle's papers.

Charlotte.

(*with the paper in her hand*)　This?

Madame Fiquet.

Oh dear, how stupid you are! The bill, don't you see? An antedated bill, in Rabourdin's name.

Charlotte.

Oh, madame, how clever that is—(*aside*) cleverer than you yourself imagine. Have no fear, the bill is safe here. (*She slips the bill into her dress.*)

Madame Fiquet.

Good! (*Looking towards Madame Vaussard*) And what does my cousin say?

Charlotte.

She is radiant. She thinks she is the heiress. (*She goes towards the door* c.)

Madame Vaussard.

(*stopping her and lowering her voice*) What was my cousin saying to you?

Charlotte.

She fancies herself the heiress. The good lady is so happy about it! (*She goes once more towards the door; then she returns, and stands between the two women.*) I beseech you, ladies, not to leave this room.

Madame Vaussard.

Ah! And why?

Charlotte.

Promise me not to tell. The will is in here.

Madame Fiquet.

In here! Where?

Charlotte.

In the safe.

Madame Vaussard.

But the key was lost.

Charlotte.

The key has been found. I tell you all this out
of kindness—I know you will not make a bad use
of it. The key is still under my poor godfather's
pillow.

Madame Fiquet.

Under the head of the——

Madame Vaussard.

(*echoing her*) Under the head——

Charlotte.

Yes, silence and respect! (*She goes up stage.
The two women turn round to follow her with their
eyes; and when she is on the threshold, before going
out, she lifts her hand, with a burlesque gesture of
authority.*)

SCENE IX.

MADAME VAUSSARD,   MADAME FIQUET.

Madame Fiquet.

(R, *aside*) That vixen of an Olympe, who reckons
on her legacy!

Madame Vaussard.

(L, *aside*) That old shrew of a Lisbeth, who flatters
herself that she is the heiress!

Madame Fiquet.

(*stepping forward; aloud, ironically*) My dear
cousin, accept my congratulations.

Madame Vaussard.

(*coming forward, same business*) My dear cousin, I
offer you mine.

Madame Fiquet.

I am delighted that our uncle has known how to reward your rare good qualities.

Madame Vaussard.

I am charmed that he made up his mind to repay your long devotion.

Madame Fiquet.

But no, cousin, it is you who are the heiress.

Madame Vaussard.

No, cousin, you are the legatee—there is no doubt about that.

Madame Fiquet.

(*crossing* R, *aside*)   She irritates me.

Madame Vaussard.

(L, *aside*)   She is too tiresome.

Madame Fiquet.

(*returning, growing angry by degrees*)   I will admit for the moment that I am the legatee.

Madame Vaussard.

(*returning, same business*)   You are too modest—but I will admit with you that the will is in my favour.

Madame Fiquet.

Perhaps I might find in myself sufficient merit to justify our uncle's choice.

Madame Vaussard.

I might discover, without too much trouble, the good qualities which I have to thank for this flattering distinction.

Madame Fiquet.
The money is left to me—do you understand, cousin ?

Madame Vaussard.
(*crossing* R, *in a fury*) You understand as well as I do, cousin, that it comes to me !

Madame Fiquet.
To you? Leave off! I have had the will read to me, word for word.

Madame Vaussard.
You ? That's a fine story ! I know the will by heart !

Madame Fiquet.
(*pointing to the door of the bedroom*) Do you want proofs ?

Madame Vaussard.
(*following her*) I was about to offer them to you. (*Madame Fiquet quickly goes into the room, while Madame Vaussard waits at the door. The first comes out again almost immediately, looking terrified, holding the key in her hand.*) Well ?

Madame Fiquet.
(*leaning against the door*) Nothing, only the shock. (*Recovering*) How childish ! (*Approaching the safe*) I know how it works.

Madame Vaussard.
(*getting behind her*) There are often loaded pistols in those safes.

Madame Fiquet.
If you are afraid, go away. (*Turns the key in the lock.*) Ah! there! (*She pushes away Madame*

Vaussard, who stretches out her hands)   Gently.
We must swear not to touch a franc, whatever may
be the contents of the will.

Madame Vaussard.

(*feverishly*)   Yes, yes, I swear—anything you like.
(*Religiously*)   What radiancy awaits our eyes!
What glorious splendour!

Madame Fiquet.

(*Passionately, holding the safe in her arms*)   My god,
my good, my all!   (*She gently rolls open the door of
the safe.   Both stand silent an instant, in an attitude
of profound devotion.   Then, little by little, they take
alarm.*)

Madame Vaussard.
Eh?

Madame Fiquet.
What is it?

Madame Vaussard.
Am I struck blind?

Madame Fiquet.
I see nothing!

Madame Vaussard.
No ray of light!   A pit of darkness!

Madame Fiquet.
A cavern as dark as an oven.

Madame Vaussard.
(*fumbling with her hands*)   But the safe is empty!

Madame Fiquet.
(*same business*)   Empty!   The safe is empty!

Madame Vaussard.

(*same business*)   Nothing on the shelves!

Madame Fiquet.

(*same business*)   Nothing in the corners!

Madame Vaussard.

(*crossing the stage* R)   Swept clean!

Madame Fiquet.

Robbed! (*She searches again, and utters a cry as she finds the ledger.*)   Ah! (*She returns up stage.*)

Madame Vaussard.

(*going after her, and stopping her*)   Show me. Don't put a thing in your pocket, or I shall call out murder! (*She brings her down to the footlights.*)

Madame Fiquet.

Let me be, I don't wish to rob myself. It must be all in bank-notes.

Madame Vaussard.

In bank-notes and title-deeds.   Let me look!

Madame Fiquet.

Don't push me like that! There, we will look at it quietly. (*Madame Fiquet opens the ledger. Madame Vaussard stands on tiptoe behind her in order to see better.*)

Madame Vaussard.

There is some writing on the first page.

Madame Fiquet.

(*reading*)   " This is my will——"

Madame Vaussard.

(*repeating after her*)   " My will——"

Madame Fiquet.

(*continuing*) " I die deeply touched by the devoted cares that have been lavished upon me by the hands of my friends." (*Interrupting herself*) That is meant for me. That good uncle! Well, cousin, are you satisfied? The legacy is mine!

Madame Vaussard.

(*snatching the ledger from her, and reading in her turn*) " I cannot feel too grateful for the atmosphere of good company which their amiable society has thrown about my death-bed." (*Interrupting herself*) That worthy uncle! That is intended for me, I should think. What did I tell you, cousin? The legacy is mine.

Madame Fiquet.

(*grasping the ledger, which Madame Vaussard continues to hold by one corner*) " And as I propose in no way to wrong my heirs, I have drawn up here the exact list of their presents." Is he making fun of us?

Madame Vaussard.

(*drawing the ledger to her, while Madame Fiquet keeps hold of one corner of it*) " In order to show the balance between what they took from me and what I was able to get back from them——" Oh Lord!

Both.

(*each holding the ledger at one side, reading together*) " I am ruined, and I leave them what they still owe me."

Madame Vaussard.

Taken in like a child! (*Going towards the door of the bedroom*) You deceitful uncle! (*Comes down stage, and takes the ledger from Madame Fiquet.*)

Madame Fiquet.

Duped! That I should be duped! (*Going to the door of the bedroom*) You wretched uncle! (*She comes down stage.*)

Madame Vaussard.

(*turning the leaves of the ledger*) What extravagance! How I regret it! My name everywhere!

Madame Fiquet.

(*glancing over the ledger*) My name on every page! (*Going to the door of the bedroom, while Madame Vaussard throws the ledger on the sofa*) And he waited till he was dead before he spoke, the coward! Ah, if I had him here! (*A violent sneeze is heard in the next room. The two women, very frightened, huddle together.*) Eh? What was that?

Madame Vaussard.

A strange noise. Somebody sneezed. (*Another and still louder sneeze.*)

Madame Fiquet.

But he is not even dead! Let us go in. (*She rushes into the room, followed by Madame Vaussard. They both return holding Rabourdin by one hand. He is dressed only in a pair of trousers falling over his feet, and with a handkerchief on his head.*)

SCENE X.

MADAME VAUSSARD, RABOURDIN, MADAME
FIQUET.

Madame Fiquet.

(*drawing him to her*) Ah! So that is all we were to find after your death!

Rabourdin.

(out of breath, beseechingly)   My kind Lisbeth——

Madame Vaussard.

(pulling him to her)   Ah!   So the safe was empty, and you were making fools of us!

Rabourdin.

My dear Olympe——

Madame Fiquet.

(same business)   You allow yourself to be petted for ten long years!

Rabourdin.

Listen to me!

Madame Vaussard.

(same business)   We load you with presents!

Rabourdin.

Let me explain——

Madame Fiquet.

How do you think I am going to marry my daughter now?

Madame Vaussard.

How do you mean me to pay my debts?

Rabourdin.

For the love of heaven—Lisbeth!   Olympe!

Madame Fiquet.

No, no.   Ah! you want Louis Quinze clocks!— and I pay for them, like a fool!

Madame Vaussard.

Ah! you want a fine funeral—three hundred francs for candles, five hundred francs for the poor!

Rabourdin.

No, not at all.　If you knew——

Madame Fiquet.

You wanted the clock to strike your last hour!

Madame Vaussard.

You have had yourself embalmed at my expense!

Rabourdin.

(*growing angry*)　But not a bit.　Damme! let me speak——

Madame Fiquet.

(*leaving go of his hand and pushing him away*)　Hold your tongue!　You have been promising us to die too long.　You're dead!

Madame Vaussard.

(*pushing him away*)　Our uncle is dead—we have no uncle!

Rabourdin.

(*beseeching them in turns*)　Come, make friends, my kind nieces.　The little presents——

Madame Fiquet.

No more presents, do you understand?

Rabourdin.

The little presents——

Madame Vaussard.

Never again, never again!

Madame Fiquet.

I'm going to take away what belongs to me.　(*She crosses and goes up stage* L.)　Wait, all that I can find.

Madame Vaussard.

I too.   (*She crosses and goes up stage* R.)

Madame Fiquet.

First the corkscrew and the box of tea-spoons.
(*She takes them from the occasional table and puts
them in her pocket.*)

Rabourdin.

(*running after her*)   Lisbeth !   Ah ! no, I say !

Madame Vaussard.

(*before the sideboard*)   The napkin-ring—the plated
dish.   (*She puts them in her pocket.*)

Rabourdin.

(*leaving Madame Fiquet to run after Madame Vaussard*)
Olympe, will you leave that alone ?   Presents are
sacred.   (*She crosses* R.)

Madame Fiquet.

(*who has come down stage, crossing* L, *going towards
the sofa*)   The cushion, under my arm.   (*Going to
the sideboard*)   The liqueur-stand, under the other
arm.

Rabourdin.

(*leaving Madame Vaussard to run after Madame
Fiquet*)   Have done, Lisbeth !   I will not let you
go.   (*He bars the door with his body.*)

Madame Vaussard.

(*loading herself with objects*)   The tray, the chair,
and the flower-stand.

Rabourdin.

(*pursuing her*)   No stupid jokes, Olympe !   You
will end by breaking something.

Madame Fiquet.

(R) Let me see, I have still one hand free. (*Looking about her, and perceiving the barometer hanging on the wall*) Ah! the barometer! (*She takes it down.*)

Rabourdin.

(*pursuing her*) My barometer!

Madame Vaussard.

(*escaping*) Good-bye, uncle! (*Rabourdin spins round without being able to catch her.*)

Madame Fiquet.

(*escaping*) Good-bye, uncle! (*Same business on the part of Rabourdin.*)

Rabourdin.

(*on the threshold*) Thieves! thieves! Help! stop them! (*He returns staggering*) Ah! wretch that I am, they are ruining me! I am ruined, ruined, ruined! I have no heirs left! (*He lets himself fall into a chair* R, *lamenting. Charlotte, who has witnessed the end of this scene from the kitchen door, enters screaming with laughter.*)

SCENE XI.

RABOURDIN, CHARLOTTE.

Rabourdin.

Ruined! It's you, you little vixen, who have ruined me!

Charlotte.

(*letting herself fall into a chair near the sofa, seizea with a violent fit of laughter*) Let me laugh! It is so good to laugh!

Rabourdin.

No more presents, no more petting, nothing.
Ah! I did not give you leave to ill-treat them so
badly as that!   You have torn my heirs to pieces.

Charlotte.

Laugh, godfather !

Rabourdin.

I have lost everything.   They will never come
back.

Charlotte.

(*rising*) What, they ?   That's a fine story !   I will
bring them back to you, humble, penitent, and
fond.

Rabourdin.

(*rising*)   You ?

Charlotte.

Yes, and at once, if you like.   Bless my soul,
what would become of them, your heirs, if they were
no longer the heirs of Rabourdin ?   Senlis would
point its finger at them ; no one would take off his
hat to them, no one would respect them, no one
would trust them.   Don't you see that their only
social position lies in their expectations from you?
Why, they can't go and put themselves into the
streets !

Rabourdin.

My niece Vaussard was very furious.

Charlotte.

Bah ! she won't know what to say to her creditors
You are her only security.

Rabourdin.

I have never seen my niece Fiquet in such a rage.

Charlotte.

And how does she expect to marry her daughter? You are that child's dowry. (*Going up stage*) They are not far off. They don't know how to come back. I will bring them back to you, I tell you. (*She beckons to them.*) Here they are!

Rabourdin.

Ah! I want to be spoilt a little. (*He puts on a dressing-gown which lies thrown over a chair, and sits down* R.)

SCENE XII.

THE FORMER, MADAME FIQUET, MADAME VAUSSARD, later EUGENIE, LEDOUX, and ISAAC

Charlotte.

(*low to Madame Vaussard, who comes in awkwardly and ill at ease, helping her to put down the things she is carrying*) You were wrong, madame. Monsieur Isaac is there. Take care—I would swear that your cousin is preparing to eat up your uncle with caresses before five minutes are over.

Madame Vaussard.

I dare say I am as clever as she is. (*She goes and fetches a cushion from the sofa.*)

Charlotte.

(*low to Madame Fiquet, who comes in : same business*) What, madame, a woman with your genius! Don't let anything get about. Think of your little girl.

9

Monsieur Ledoux is there. (*Pointing to Madame Vaussard, who is going up to Rabourdin with a cushion in her hand.*) There, look at your cousin. She has started codling him already.

Madame Fiquet.

(*looking at the cushion which Charlotte is taking from her*) Well, well. I never ceased to love our dear uncle. (*Rushes towards Rabourdin, and reaches him just in time to place the cushion which she has brought back behind his back. Madame Vaussard looks about to see what she can do with the one she is holding in her hand, and ends by placing it under her uncle's feet.*)

Isaac.

(*entering*) What ! is he up ? (*Madame Vaussard, ill at ease, leads him aside* R.) You will at least keep up your payments regularly ?

Madame Vaussard.

(*low*) Hush ! Fie ! to talk of that when you see that I am still in tears. Later on !

Ledoux.

(*entering with Eugénie*) Getting better already ! (*Madame Fiquet, frightened, keeps him back, up stage* L.) And the wedding, and my twelve hundred francs ?

Madame Fiquet.

(*low*) Hush ! It's disgraceful, when our uncle, whom we love so dearly, is restored to us by a miracle. Later on. (*Madame Vaussard returns to Rabourdin, behind whom stand Madame Fiquet and Eugénie. Ledoux and Isaac are up stage, one* R, *the other* L. *Charlotte, leaning against the sofa, smiles as she observes the scene.*)

Rabourdin.

(*stammering*) I am touched, very deeply touched, my children.

SCENE XIII.

Mourgue.

(*holding a toothpick, which he uses between each sentence*) Dear! dear! dear! That rogue of a Rabourdin. Nature is a wonderful doctor. She has such depths. I dined like a god this evening. (*Goes up to Rabourdin.*)

Dominique.

(*to Charlotte, low*) Here comes Chapuzot.

Charlotte.

(*going towards Chapuzot, who comes forward painfully on two sticks, and leading him* R, *preventing him from seeing Rabourdin*) What has happened to you, dear monsieur?

Chapuzot.

Nothing, nothing. A false step. I fell down. They carried me home. I would have crawled back on my knees rather than stay away. Here are the three hundred francs. Put them away.

Charlotte.

(*taking the notes, and putting them into her dress*) They are quite safe.

Chapuzot.

(*going up to Rabourdin*) What do I see? He has

come to life again! (*Runs after Charlotte*) Give me my three hundred francs.

Charlotte.

(*low*) Hush! How troublesome you are. Later on.

Mourgue.

(*holding Rabourdin's pulse*) Capital! The quieting medicine was no good : we must try a black draught.

Chapuzot.

(*seated on the sofa, aside*) I will wait. (*Aloud*) When the hulk is worth nothing, doctor, it is better that it should go down without delay—eh, Rabourdin? (*He rises and joins the group standing about Rabourdin.*)

Rabourdin.

(*rising, coming down to the footlights, followed by the heirs*) Yes, old friend, yes. I ask for nothing better than to pass away, on a peaceful evening, surrounded by you all, in the bosom of my family.

Charlotte,

(*showing the money to Dominique,* R, *where they make a separate couple*) And now, as soon as the priest is ready!

CURTAIN.

Printed by Hazell, Watson, & Viney, Ld., London and Aylesbury.